THE BILLIONAIRE'S MARRIAGE BARTER

MELODY ARCHER

BOOK REVIEWS

"This was a very moving and enjoyable story. It was so captivating I couldn't put it down till I finished it. If you like exciting, moving, sweet clean romances you will enjoy reading this story." -Shadowell

"Luke and Razelle will have you wanting them to make it to a happily ever after. Luke and Razelle both have experienced hardship and pain.

Luke used his grief to live a better life out on his grandfather's property and gave up on relationships. This is also his problem because in order to inherit the property he has to marry and that timeframe is quickly approaching.

Razelle's life is closely that of an indentured servant. Her mother controls all aspects of her life making Razelle miserable.

A chance encounter followed by close communication will turn their lives around and secrets will come out that will change lives even more. This story will have you glued to the pages waiting in anticipation as this story unfolds." -Merry

"And at last, I see the light, and it's like the sky is new. And its warm and real and bright, and the world has somehow shifted..." *Rapunzel (from the movie)*

CHAPTER ONE

uke

"How can I help you?" The young woman behind the counter of Angelique's Cafe, spoke in a gentle voice that drew him in.

But it was her large green eyes and her upturned nose sprinkled with freckles that captivated him.

Thick auburn hair weaved into braids encircled her head like a halo and only added to that girl-next-door look that he loved.

Luke Stevenson didn't realize he was staring at the woman until she cleared her throat.

It wasn't only her beauty that captured his attention. Luke was sure he'd seen her before.

"S... ssorry, I was thinking." He stuttered. Suddenly he

remembered his brother Gabe's wedding and it all came back to him. "Aren't you Rory Stevenson's friend?"

Her cheeks blossomed into a lovely shade of red. "Um, yes Razelle. And you're Gabe's brother Luke Stevenson, right?"

"Guilty." Luke mentally kicked himself that he stuttered the first time he talked to her in months. He tilted his head slightly to the side with a half-smile on his face.

The corners of her lips turned up for a moment until suddenly interrupted by a woman's high-pitched voice. She called Razelle's name from the kitchen.

Razelle turned her head and answered. "Just a minute. I'll be right there." She looked back to him and asked. "My Mother needs my help in the back. If you can tell me your order, I'll get started on it right away."

"I'll get a coffee and a half dozen blueberry muffins. And I'll take that to go." Luke paid for his order and watched as she poured his coffee. As she handed it to him she said. "I'll bring the muffins to you as soon as I can."

"Sure. No hurry." Luke carried his coffee and set it on a table in the corner. Sounds of chatter along with the hum of coffee machines filled the cafe. Men and women sat together at tables sipping their coffee, smiling and chatting together.

While waiting, his phone dinged with a text from his brother. He texted Gabe back letting him know he'd call in an hour. He didn't like to talk on his phone when he was surrounded by a bunch of people. His brother could wait.

Meanwhile, he looked around the old fashioned cafe.

This two story building was located on a little known

street in their small town of Paradise Lake. It bordered a country road. Most folks on the other side of town referred to this area as the poor side.

But this little coffee shop was very cute.

It had an old-world feel to it that he was sure his mother and grandmother would love.

When he'd parked his truck outside he'd noticed the blue and white striped awning that covered the sidewalk and the hanging flowering plants that hung along the windowsill.

Inside the cafe, the tables and matching chairs had a 1950s charm that reminded him of watching reruns of the TV show Happy Days. He would need to bring his Mom and GrandMom to this coffee shop. They'd love it.

"Here you go." Razelle set a large box on the table. The smell of freshly baked muffins wafted up his nose.

"They smell so good."

"Just came out of the oven." Razelle looked over at him, her big green eyes were made larger by her wan appearance. She had dark circles under her eyes that he hadn't noticed before. He wondered what caused her sleepless nights.

Maybe he would need to get to know her well enough to ask.

Luke looked up at her. "Thanks for this. Now that I know where your coffee shop is, I'll need to stop by more often." He stood to his feet right next to Razelle. His shoulder bumped lightly against hers and she stepped backwards swaying a little on her feet. Luke slipped an arm around her waist to stop her from falling.

Her strawberry lips captivated him and he wanted to pull her close and kiss her senseless.

Scared at the desire that suddenly rose up inside of him, he helped steady her before quickly removing his arm.

"Thanks for that. I'm not usually this clumsy." Raz grimaced and shook her head slightly.

A wavy tendril of auburn hair fell loose from the braid that encircled her head. It was so silky, that Luke itched to run his hand through her hair. He would love to see her hair loose and hanging down her back. It would be beautiful.

He shifted on his feet, feeling heat rising from his neck to his cheeks. He needed to change the direction of his thoughts.

"Are you okay?" It was as close as Luke would allow himself to ask about the dark circles under her eyes.

"I'm good. It's been a long day. I think I just need a good sleep tonight." Razelle gave him a small smile. "Well, I should go. Enjoy the muffins."

"I look forward to them." Luke's gaze lingered a little longer. "It was good to see you again Razelle. I'll see you next time."

"Okay." She nodded and walked back to her place behind the counter. Before long, she was helping another customer.

Luke forced himself not to look at her again as he left the coffee shop.

As he got into his truck and drove away, his thoughts still lingered on the beautiful coffee shop girl. He wasn't sure why he couldn't stop thinking of her. He'd had many opportunities to meet beautiful women, but Razelle seemed different somehow.

As he parked his truck beside the cabin on Grand's land, he did his best to shake off thoughts about her.

There was no way he was dating or falling in love.

He'd already played that hand and failed.

Luke carried his coffee and muffins into the house before hauling the wood and tools he bought at the hardware store off the back of the truck. Soon he had everything he needed on the deck.

Fixing up the deck that wrapped around the cabin was to be his last project before this old place would be completely renovated.

Luke had started it last year when he moved out here. He'd done everything by himself and he was quite happy with the result.

His arm trembled as he held the length of the solid wood. With the other hand he gripped the hammer, swinging it onto the nail he held in place. This was the last portion of the porch he needed to fix up then he'd be satisfied that this old cabin was renovated close to its original design.

It was still morning and he wanted to get as much done as he could today to finish this project.

Sweat rolled down his forehead, reminding him of those three years he'd worked as a roustabout in Boone Donovan's Texas Oil Company. He'd worked his way up the ranks until he had become Boone's right hand man.

It had been the perfect job for him.

He had wanted a job that didn't require him to talk much. The stuttering had begun right after his Dad died.

Students had teased him mercilessly throughout his school years. Luckily, his mom had taken him to a speech pathologist in Middle School. Since then, he stuttered only on rare occasions.

But, he was glad enough to work with his hands, or work with numbers.

Luke was good at both and neither of those skills required much talking.

Without warning, the shrill sound of his cell phone rang through the open window.

Opening the screen door, he hurried through the house to where his phone lay on the kitchen table.

"Luke here."

"Hey man. Sounds like you're out of breath. What's up?" It was good to hear his brother Gabe's voice. Even though he'd seen his family a week ago at a charity event, he was always happy to chat with one of his brothers.

"Just fixing the porch on the cabin. Almost finished." Luke tipped his head back, enjoying a long drink from his water bottle.

"Are you enjoying life out at Grand's old lake cabin?"

Luke set down the water bottle on the kitchen table. "Yeah. It's been good to leave the rush of the city to try the quiet life for a while."

"That cabin is pretty much falling apart. Doesn't that place still have the original wood that Grand used to build it in the 1920s?" Gabe's voice held a note of surprise on the other end of the phone line.

Luke chuckled at the concern he heard in his brother's voice. "Don't worry, Gabe. The place isn't falling down around me. At least not yet, anyway. I've fixed up the inside of the cabin. Now I'm just working on completing the deck."

Luke continued. "This place might be out of the way, but I've grown to like it here. It's quiet and helps you get back to the simple pleasures of life."

"You've been there now for eleven months?"

"Yes. I only have two weeks left before I'm free of the tight budgeting restrictions I placed on myself for the past year."

"Well, you did that for a good cause and from what I've heard, it seems like your followers have really appreciated what you've done. You've been a great role model for them to follow. I've seen so many great comments."

Luke's memories went back to a year ago when he had decided on a whim that he would limit his personal budget to the monthly income of the average American, and that he would commit to do this for a full year. It had turned out well.

"Yeah, people have told me that it's inspired them to watch their spending and to learn to save and budget their finances. That was really encouraging to hear. That was my goal when I started this. I hope it continues to help more people."

"Dad would be pleased at what you've done here."

Tears pricked the back of his eyes, as he thought of his father. Luke blinked them back. "Too bad he d... ddied so early." Luke heard himself stutter. He cringed to hear himself. It always happened when his emotions ran high.

"I know man." Gabe sighed heavily on the other end of the phone. "At least we've done our best to make some good out of it."

"Yeah." Luke sighed remembering. "I've told my students our story. They know that a big reason I have a passion to help others is because of the struggles our family went through."

"Thanks to Dad's dishonest business partner." Gabe muttered.

"True. But that's why I'm also doing my best to teach people how to set up their business partnerships carefully so they aren't in trouble later." Luke ran a hand through his hair as he remembered the terrible time in their family's life when their father's business partner had stolen his money.

"I sss..still miss him." Luke whispered and swallowed back emotions that threatened to choke him.

Both brothers were silent for a few moments as memories surfaced of their Dad's heart attack and death a few days later.

"I know. We all do. But, I think Dad would be pleased that something meant for evil was turned around and used for good. That's what you're doing Luke, when you help others." Gabe's words were like a soothing balm to Luke.

"I hope so. I'm working on it." Luke expelled a breath.

Gabe chuckled softly and spoke. "Now it looks like there's only one thing left for you to do."

"What's that?" Luke walked over to the large window that overlooked the thousand acre property.

"Fulfill the terms of Grand's will so you can inherit that land and live there, permanently. Your twenty-seventh birthday is just around the corner."

Luke began to pace at Gabe's reminder of Great-

Grandfather's will requirement for each of his great-grandsons. He only had five weeks until his twenty-seventh birthday. According to Grand's will, he needed to be married by then if he wanted to inherit this piece of land.

Anxiety sat heavy in the pit of his stomach.

"I know, I know. The deadline is staring me in the face."

"You still want all those acres of land Grand planned for you to inherit?"

"You know I do." Luke stared across the land seeing a few oil derricks pumping in the distance. Yes, he wanted this land. He wanted it with every fiber of his being. He'd dreamed of owning it, ever since his Great Grandfather brought him here as a young boy.

Of course back then, there were a dozen horses and cattle on the land as well. Luke remembered being so sad when Grand had sold off all the horses and cattle in the last couple of years before he died. Grand had chosen to live his final years on the homestead property, the place his brother Adam had inherited.

But, this thousand acre spread of land had remained fallow. The only activity on the land for the last ten years had been those two oil derricks that had continued to pump oil and produce a steady income.

A passion had been sparked in his childhood, that someday he would own this land. Luke wanted to build a sprawling ranch house here. He would bring back the horses and cattle and continue to keep the oil derricks running at the far end of the land.

The only thing missing in his life was a wife and children. Memories haunted him and put a sour taste in his mouth regarding love and marriage.

He refused to go through the heartbreak of falling in love again.

"There's one small problem. I haven't been dating anyone, Gabe. I've basically sworn off women ever since Audra left me at the altar."

His brother expelled a breath. "You're going to have to let that go, Luke. Besides, not all women are like your ex-fiance."

"Maybe." Luke wasn't convinced that was true. His belief probably explained why he hadn't dated seriously since.

Gabe continued. "Well, you could always consider a marriage of convenience. It turned out well for your older brothers."

"Back-fired you mean. All three of you fell in love." Luke muttered, his belly fisting into a tight knot at the thought of being spurned by a woman, yet again. He wasn't about to go through that emotional turmoil again, not if he could help it.

"Hey man, don't discount the power of love. I'm living proof that love can come to you when you least expect it."

Luke was resolute. "I'm glad you're happy, Gabe. But as far as I'm concerned, love isn't for me."

"What about your inheritance?"

"I'll consider a marriage in-name-only. I'm afraid that will be the only way I'll agree to Grand's crazy plan." Luke set his jaw in a firm line determined not to be played for a fool by another woman again.

"All right, man. I can't wait to meet her." Gabe's teasing chuckle echoed through the phone line.

Luke grunted in response. "Well, don't hold your breath. I'm not sure there's a woman out there who will agree to this ridiculous idea."

Just as soon as the words were out of his mouth, his thoughts turned to the beautiful woman he'd seen in the coffee shop today.

Razelle.

She was charming and kind.

His brother interrupted his musings.

"She's out there. I'm confident of that. Sweet dreams brother." Gabe was still chuckling as he ended the call.

Luke set his phone down on the kitchen table and stared out the window, expelling a frustrated sigh. The orange hue of the sun setting behind the trees and the oil derricks in the distance was a sight that stirred his dreams.

He couldn't deny he was desperate to make this land his own.

The conversation with his brother sparked a deeper hunger — and if he were honest — a newfound surrender to the possibility of a marriage of convenience.

He would do whatever it took to make this land his own.

Even if it meant, marrying a fake wife.

A knot formed in his belly at the decision.

He was sure all sorts of things would go wrong. But it's what he needed to do.

CHAPTER TWO

azelle

RAZ SIGHED HEAVILY and locked the door to the cafe after the last customer left for the day.

Her thoughts still lingered on the handsome man who came into the coffee shop today.

Luke Stevenson.

He was quiet, brooding and far too handsome for his own good, especially wearing that Stetson on his head.

She had always secretly loved that rugged, cowboy look on a man. Maybe it was because it reminded her of living in the country and having a permanent place to call home.

Having a home and the love and belonging that went with it was something she'd always dreamed of, even as a little girl.

Seeing Luke this morning, reminded her of those dreams.

It was something she didn't believe she'd ever have.

Her mother's rules made that impossible.

Sighing heavily, Razelle walked to the kitchen to grab her cleaning supplies.

The other two baristas had already left for the day and it was time to get the rest of her chores done.

Mother didn't like to pay workers overtime, so everyday it was up to her to clean the dining area and kitchen in their coffee shop.

"You'll need to help Miguel clean up the food and wipe down the kitchen, clean the counter, table tops and mop the floors." Mother stood behind the counter top by the cash register. The shuttering sound of the till tape being printed filled the room. As usual, Mother was busy balancing the books and counting the money made that day.

"Of course, Mother." Razelle knew her job and felt like she didn't need to be reminded every night. But her mother demanded that all the details of her world be controlled. Which meant that her daughter had to meet Mother's exacting standards or there would be trouble.

Razelle hurried to the kitchen to help Miguel clean up.

"Missy Raz, I already packaged the extra food for today. And I'll wipe the kitchen countertops. You go ahead and clean the dining area." Miguel was their short order cook who worked during the weekdays. He had always been very helpful.

"Miguel, you're so nice to me. Thank you." Razelle bent

down under the sink and grabbed the disinfectant spray and the stack of wipes.

"You're easy to be nice too, missy." Miguel grinned and whispered. "Also, don't forget the blue container in the fridge. You take it with you tonight."

"Thanks so much. It means a lot." A tear escaped out of one eye as she looked into his brown eyes filled with kindness.

Miguel knew that in the past year she went once a week to the camp that was located across the creek and down in the valley. She brought food and herbal remedies to help with those who were hungry and sick. Miguel had kept her secret ever since he had found food missing from his kitchen.

Her mother didn't know. It had to stay that way.

Helping people at the camp was important to Raz. She wanted to do something for them.

When her friend Cassie had asked her to come with her to the camp one night a year ago, she had gone. And had been shocked at the lack of food and by how many people were sick.

She'd decided then and there that she would go every week and bring what supplies she could to help.

"Of course. And make sure you still get some sleep tonight."

"I will, I promise." Razelle smiled at him and carried the cleaning supplies to the cafe area. She worked quickly and got all her work done in record time.

Her mother looked over her work as usual and nodded.

"My head is bothering me tonight." Mother said as they climbed the stairs to their apartment above Angelique's Cafe. She was thankful they didn't have to walk very far to get home. When her mother had bought this place three years ago, it had seemed like the perfect place. Finally, they wouldn't be moving from place to place almost every year, like they had done all her life.

But her mother continued to have headaches. She always had tension headaches as far back as Razelle could remember. When she turned eight, Raz started to learn how to massage her Mother's head and back to take away the pain.

"If you lie down on your bed, I'll get the cream and be back soon." It was her duty to help her Mother feel better. She handed her mother some pain medicine and after she swallowed it back, Razelle began massaging her Mother's head in gentle circles to soothe the pain.

She hoped it wouldn't take too long for her mother to fall asleep. There was still so much to get ready for tonight.

After only fifteen minutes, the sound of her Mother's steady snores echoed across the room.

Raz breathed a sigh of relief.

Tiptoeing out of the bedroom, Raz went to the kitchen to find food. She hadn't eaten anything since breakfast, and her stomach was protesting. Her white fluff-ball cat, Sunbeam, was meowing asking for cat food. Raz quickly opened a can and placed it in her bowl.

She ate a sandwich and ran her fingers through her cat's thick white fur. Her purring sounds helped Raz relax.

After she was finished, she hurried to her bedroom.

Closing the door behind her she changed out of her work clothes into jeans and t-shirt. She filled her backpack with dried herbs, that she'd grown herself. They had proven useful for natural healing of fevers and other sickness.

She went to the kitchen in the coffee shop to grab the container filled with food. Hurrying back upstairs she shoved everything she needed for tonight inside her backpack.

After slipping on her hoodie and running shoes, she quietly opened her window and climbed out. Careful to close the window, she climbed down the roof until she reached the tall, sturdy poplar tree that stood outside her window.

Scurrying down the tree she was soon on the ground. She hurried along the trail toward the river. It was dark outside except for the street lights from their small town.

She took out her flashlight to guide her way.

Crossing the river in her small rowboat, soon she made it to the other side and hurried toward the camp.

With silent steps she made her way toward the ramshackle cabin where they kept a few medical supplies. Her best friend Cassie said she'd meet her here. Her friend had a big heart for others.

After she discovered a few teenagers from the camp a little over a year ago, she'd made it her mission to help them and had talked Razelle into going with her.

Raz quietly opened the door to the cabin and was greeted with a hug.

Addy clung to her longer than usual and when Raz stepped back, the teenager's eyes were filled with worry. "I'm so glad you're here."

"Of course I'm here. I said I'd come." Raz looked at Addy and then to Cassie and fear rose in her belly at the anxiousness in her friend's eyes. "What's happened?"

"The man that Ryan brought here yesterday, he's sick. He's got a fever. I'm not sure what's wrong with him." Cassie pointed to the cot at the far end of the cabin where the man lay tossing and turning in a feverish sleep.

Raz walked over to him and set her backpack on the floor before she touched his forehead.

He was burning hot.

"Cassie, we need to bring his temperature down. I'm going to do my best to cool his body. And if you could boil water to make herbal tea that would be helpful." Razelle began, taking charge with what she could do to help.

Cassie started the camping stove that sat on the small table near the door. She filled the kettle from the large five gallon pails they kept filled in the cabin. The stove was powered by gasoline, so it didn't need electricity or propane to run. It was one of the few items that Sloane — the leader of the camp — had allowed them to have in this cabin.

Soon the water boiled and Razelle pulled the small bag of feverfew herbs out of her backpack. After she'd made a cup of the herb tea, she allowed time for the steaming cup to cool before she spoon-fed it to the man.

The sick man moaned as Raz lifted his head to drink. He sipped only a little tea, but she hoped it would be enough to help lower his fever.

Cassie, Addy and Razelle continued to watch over him for the rest of the night until they could see the red glow of dawn in the sky.

"I've got to get going. I can't be late getting home, or Mother will find out I've been gone." Raz left behind the food and herbs, but grabbed the containers and put them inside her backpack. She didn't want Mother to find out her containers were missing.

"I know. But it would be so helpful if you could stay. That man's fever isn't low enough yet." Cassie and Addy walked with her outside the cabin and down toward the creek.

Razelle sighed. "You know I wish I could stay. Addy, you can help Cassie take care of that sick man today alright?"

"Yes. I know what to do." Addy pushed back her sandy blonde hair away and wrapped her arms around her belly.

"There you see? Addy will help. You'll be fine." Raz gave her friends hugs, wishing she wouldn't have to leave for home so soon.

❦

"LUKE." A man's voice growled loudly outside his cabin door accompanied by several loud knocks. Luke rolled over in bed and stared at the clock on his nightstand.

It was only four in the morning. Who could be banging on his door at this early hour?

"Come on, Luke. Open the door! It's Hudson."

Groaning, he sat up rolling his legs over the side of the bed and rubbed his eyes.

The last time his best friend had knocked on his door early in the morning was when they were in High School and Hudson's mom had needed to be rushed to the hospital for heart problems.

"Hold on, man." Concerned, Luke hurried to pull on jeans, slipped on a t-shirt and raced to the door.

Throwing open the door his friend stood there staring at him, silent. Hudson ran a hand through his auburn hair while dark brows puckered together forming deep worry lines on his forehead.

"Come in, Hud. You look terrible."

"Yeah." His friend stumbled through the door, his mind clearly elsewhere.

Luke eyed his friend for a moment noticing the dark circles under his bloodshot eyes. He pulled out a wooden chair from the table and pointed to it. "Sit down for a minute. Catch your breath. I'm going to make coffee. When you're ready, you can tell me what's got you all in a bother."

As his friend sank slowly into the chair, Luke walked to the kitchen counter and began to add the coffee grounds to his new coffee machine. It was the one luxury he'd allowed himself since moving to Grand's cabin.

Proving that it was possible to live below the national average household income and still save and invest his money, had been a sacrifice.

But he owed it to the people who bought his software and Smartphone Apps on budgeting and investing to show them that if he could do it, they could too.

Which was why he moved out here to this two room run-down cabin.

Almost a year ago he'd had the idea to move here to live on Grand's thousand acres. This was the same land his great-grandfather stipulated in his will that Luke was to inherit if he married by his twenty seventh birthday.

That deadline was coming way too fast.

Only Grand could get away with such a ridiculous notion.

It shouldn't have surprised him that the old coot came up with a plan to control their lives long after he went to his reward.

He had no idea where he would find a fake wife by the time his birthday came around.

Luke rubbed his eyes and turned to his best friend.

With bubbling sounds of the coffee machine percolating in the background, Luke pulled out a chair and turned it around placing his arms on the backrest.

"So tell me what's up, Hud. The only other time I've seen you this worried was when your mom had that heart attack years ago." Luke leaned his chin on his arms, fixing his gaze on his best friend.

"Well, this time it's almost as bad." Hudson lifted his head, placing his elbows on the table. For a moment, a haunted look came over his brown eyes as Hud stared at him in silence.

Luke waited.

"It's Waylon."

"Your brother?" At Hudson's nod, Luke pressed for answers. "What happened to him?"

"That's just it. I don't know. He's disappeared." Hud ran one hand through his already unkempt hair. Luke could see his hand shook slightly with the movement. "I called his phone two nights ago and I just figured he was out.

But when I called again late last night and got no answer, I stopped by his apartment. He wasn't home."

"Do you have any idea where your brother could have gone to?"

Hudson shook his head. "Not really. The few places that I thought of, I just spent all night checking those places out. He wasn't anywhere to be found."

"Hmm. And there aren't any other favorite hangout spots he's told you about?"

Hud scratched his forehead a faraway look in his eyes. "Well, there is one other place. In the past few weeks Waylon has talked about seeing some places with his friend Ryan. He kept talking about going to the camp by the creek."

"*The camp,* as in the hangout for drug dealers? You think your brother went there?" Hudson nodded, his forehead puckered in worry.

Luke could understand his friend's concern for his brother. That camp was on the other side of Grand's land by a few miles, along the long four-mile stretch of a tree line that bordered the creek.

Years ago, when Hudson and Luke were in middle school they used to spend so much time together on the weekends riding their trail motorbikes along the banks of the creek. Since Luke had returned from Texas, he learned it had become a haven for drug dealers and other illegal activities.

No wonder Hudson was worried.

"I think it's likely." Hudson sighed heavily. "As much as I don't want to, I need to see if Waylon's there. If he is, I need to bring him home before Mom has another heart attack from worry."

"Well, what are we waiting for? Let's go get your brother and bring him home." Luke stood to his feet and clapped his friend on the shoulder. Luke pulled a hoodie over his head, slipped on his shoes and opened the door.

Hudson got up from the table and followed close behind. "Thanks man. I owe you one."

Luke shrugged. "I'm happy to help. Friends look out for each other." Luke hurried to the shed where he kept two ATVs. He always kept two of everything he considered useful to his life, in case one of them broke down. This time, it would pay off.

He tossed a helmet and keys to Hudson. "We can drive up to the tree line, but then we'll need to walk from there. We don't want them to hear us coming."

"Good idea." Hudson put on his helmet and started the engine.

Luke started his ATV and drove out of the shed and across Grand's yard. Soon they were following the familiar dirt road. Hudson and Luke had driven their dirt bikes along this trail many times during high school when they went off-roading together.

He turned back with a grin at his friend, thinking of all those hot summer days they'd spent riding the back wood trails together. They had forged their own paths through the dense trees that lined the edge of Grand's land. In all their adventures along the creek during those middle school years, they knew the area well.

When they reached the tree line just beyond Grand's land, Luke stopped the ATV and turned off the engine.

Hudson was right behind him.

The morning sun was trying to poke its head above the clouds, but so far the outside world around them was muted in shades of light grey with speckles of red from the rising sun.

"We'll need to be as quiet as we can. We don't want to alert whoever is guarding the place." Luke whispered and a grimace formed on his lips as he hung his helmet on the handlebar of the four-wheeler.

Hudson chuckled ruefully as he followed. "No, I don't suppose we do. So what's the plan?"

Luke started walking through the thick maze of trees, hearing his friend's footsteps behind him.

"The only plan I have is to search through the camp to try to find your brother. We'll start looking along the border and make our way inside." Luke turned to Hudson, who nodded.

"Sounds good."

They walked for a good thirty minutes before they saw the outline of a few rundown wood cabins and makeshift tents. Clothes hung at awkward angles over ropes that had been tied between trees. Broken bicycles, old tires and extra household items were haphazardly thrown on the hard dirt between the tents.

Everything about this place looked like it was falling apart.

Luke shook his head at the sight. "Let's start at the edge of the camp over that way." He pointed to the western corner. The bubbling sounds of the creek could be heard in the background as they made their way nearer the waters edge.

Loud snores of people sleeping and the sounds of a

few children crying, could be heard throughout the camp. As they approached the creek, two women and a teenage girl stood with their heads close together. Luke overheard their whispers.

He turned to Hudson, gesturing for silence.

The woman with the thick auburn braid that hung below her waist, spoke in a hurried whisper. "Cassie, I can't stay. My mother will be very angry if she finds out I'm missing."

"I know and I'm sorry Raz. But, Rye's friend is sick. He was throwing up most of the last two nights. He needs your help and you're the only one who knows what to do." The raven haired girl's brows puckered with worry.

The teenage girl clung to the woman with the auburn hair.

"Addy, you can help Cassie take care of that sick man today alright?"

"Yes. I remember what you've taught me." The teenager pushed back sandy blonde hair away from her face and wrapped her arms around her middle.

"There you see? Addy will help. You'll be fine." The woman with the auburn hair started to move away.

Luke's ears perked up as he listened.

"You'll have to watch over him today. Sloane isn't going to let the new guy leave anyway. He'll be stuck here for awhile."

It sounded as if this guy Sloane was a leader of sorts.

"You know Sloane would do anything for you, especially after you saved his life." Cassie's voice turned desperate. "Raz please stay a little longer."

"I can't. But, I'll be back tomorrow night. Okay?" The

woman with the long braid stepped away from her friend. The teenager sighed and trembled slightly as the woman turned away.

She was intent on walking down the path to the creek, when Luke stepped in front of her.

A sudden gasp of surprise flew out of her mouth.

He froze. Here she was, standing in front of him.

The woman from the coffee shop.

Razelle.

Wide green eyes widened at the sight of him. He drank in the sight of her. She was beautiful with auburn hair that framed large green eyes, a delicate upturned nose and full lips. Dark brown lashes dusted cheeks that flushed rosy against the backdrop of the warm red glow of the sunrise.

Just as quickly, the surprised look on her face was replaced by wariness. She tucked her hands deeper in the sleeves of the large hoodie and crossed her arms across her chest.

Luke realized he'd better start talking if he wanted to keep her attention.

He stepped close enough to see her face which was shadowed by the hoodie that framed her face. She looked young and much too thin. The woman stood there as if trying to hide in the depths of her oversized clothes.

"R…Razelle." Luke hated it that he stuttered. He had seen her yesterday and something inside him insisted that he needed to impress her. He could tell that was a total failure.

A memory suddenly came back to him of when he met her at Gabe and Rory's wedding. Ever since he'd laid eyes on her the first time, he couldn't get Raz out of his mind.

That day was etched forever in his mind. Razelle had worn a cream colored off the shoulder dress that highlighted her slender figure. He still remembered her long beautiful hair had been loose that day. Thick auburn tresses had descended downward, past her waist rippling like ripened reddish-brown wheat in the sun.

She was a vision.

Her beauty was only one of the many things that attracted him. She also had a spark for life and a compassion for others that drew him to her.

She was captivating.

At the flicker of recognition that sparked in her eyes, he sighed in relief. He chided himself for being a little too elated that she remembered him.

An unexpected protectiveness welled up inside him as he stared at the woman in front of him. She was too kind, too compassionate and much too vulnerable to be side-by-side with the seedy people at this camp.

Not only that, but if the dark shadows under her eyes and her thin shivering body were any indication, she was exhausted.

What was Raz doing in this seedy place in the middle of the night, anyway?

Luke didn't know if he wanted to shake some sense into her for taking the risk, or if he just wanted to hold her close.

If he were honest with himself, he'd choose the latter.

Only he wouldn't stop there.

He'd likely kiss her senseless.

He swallowed and took a small step back.

But he wouldn't do that, not yet anyway.

As tempting as she was, at this moment what he needed most were answers. A wave of protectiveness welled up inside of him.

"What are you doing here — in this unsafe place in the middle of the night?"

CHAPTER THREE

azelle

"LUKE STEVENSON." Razelle folded her arms across her chest at his probing question.

Her brows puckered as she stared undaunted at the tall, broad shouldered man in front of her. The fact that he stuttered as he said her name, didn't bother her. She found it refreshing that this handsome man — with all his connections, money and influence — had at least one flaw.

When she'd first met Luke at her friend Rory's wedding, she'd been attracted to him and a little over-whelmed by the Stevenson family. His mother was so kind, his grandparents were fun and it seemed all five brothers had won the genetics lottery with their hand-some good looks.

It was the kind of family she'd always dreamed of being a part of ever since she was a little girl.

For as far back as she could remember, it had only ever been her Mother and her. Once in a while she had vague night dreams of being a small child cuddled by a mother who smelled like a herb garden and being tossed in the air by a father who loved to play with her.

She assumed she had those dreams because of her deep longing for a family to love.

The day when she met the Stevenson family at her friend Rory's wedding, it had reminded her of what she didn't have. It was just her Mother and her. The two of them were all family she had. But, she wouldn't bring it up with her Mother. She knew better. Raz knew her Mother would get angry if she found out there was something about their relationship that made her daughter unhappy.

Still, she couldn't help but feel a little sad about it.

If she were honest with herself, it was seeing Luke Stevenson again that reminded her of the perfect family she longed for — and it poked at the missing piece in her life.

Seeing him again yesterday and tonight annoyed her more than anything. At least she tried to convince herself of that.

She was concerned about the fact that she couldn't stop thinking about him.

It worried her more than a little.

Luke stepped closer and of a sudden she became very aware that she was staring at him.

His jawline was set in determination as he waited for her answer.

Frustrated by his probing questions, she boldly turned it back around to him. "I could ask you the same thing."

Unexpectedly, a grin turned up the corners of his mouth.

Raz had a feeling that Luke liked it when she spoke her mind.

At the moment, she didn't want to do anything to please Luke Stevenson.

He cocked his head to the side as he stared at her a moment longer before he spoke. "Fair enough."

He turned to his friend for a moment before focusing on her once more. "We're looking for someone. I overheard you two talking about some new guy who arrived at the camp."

She tore her gaze away from his and began to step away. "You shouldn't listen in on other people's conversations."

Raz's voice wobbled with weariness and if she were honest — fear.

It wasn't just that she was afraid of getting in trouble with her Mother, although that fear was very real.

If she were honest, the much bigger worry would be if she allowed herself to get close to this man. She found herself attracted to Luke and her protective instincts set off alarm bells in her head warning: *danger, danger.*

Anxiety knifed through her belly and suddenly she felt a desperate need to escape. "Sorry, I really need to go."

"Wait." Luke once again stepped in front of her. "All I'm asking for is a couple minutes of your time."

Her friend Cassie stepped toward them, looking at her then at Luke. The teenage girl huddled close to Razelle.

"You know him?" Cassie looked up at her.

Razelle hesitated before she replied. "Yes. This is Luke. His brother is married to my friend Rory." Raz looked over Luke's shoulder to the man standing behind him.

"This is a friend." Luke turned quickly to Hudson before his gaze landed on the blond haired woman.

"Hudson." His friend shook each of the ladies' hands.

"I'm Cassie, Raz's friend. This is Addy." The dark haired woman nodded at the teenager before turning back to Hudson. "You said you were looking for someone?"

Hudson's brows puckered in worry. "It's my brother. He left his apartment a few days ago and I haven't seen him since. Not sure where he is, and this is one of the last places I can think of, where I might find him."

Razelle sighed heavily.

She could hear the worry in Hudson's voice and her heart went out to him. Raz knew she wouldn't be able to leave until she brought him to see the man that was sick. Maybe he was Hudson's brother.

"All right. I'll take you to him. But then I really need to go. Follow me and keep as quiet as you can." Raz began walking up the gentle slope of the creek bank. Cassie and Addy followed closely and the men weren't far behind.

The rest of the camp was asleep and she really hoped to keep it that way — at least until Luke and his friend left.

Raz had a feeling her compassion for people who were hurt, sick or in trouble, would land her in hot water someday.

She only hoped that today wouldn't be that day.

Looking around furtively she saw no one was up and about yet. As she walked silently toward the rundown wood cabin where the man lay sick, she motioned for the others to follow.

Thunder rumbled loudly and she looked up to see dark clouds forming in the sky above.

She shivered.

Ducking under some trees, she stepped under the wooded area that led to the cabin. The scent of burning wood wafted up her nose. Thin layers of smoke arose from the wood-burning barrel near the door.

The scent of campfire triggered a pleasant memory, but it was hazy. She shook it off and opened the wobbly door slowly. Raz feared any extra noise would alert Sloane and his men so she put a finger to her lips, signalling for everyone to stay quiet.

This old cabin was a good size for one or two people and supplies, but felt cramped with all of them.

Raz had used this run down building when she had come to the camp the first time one of the children was sick. That had been about a year ago now. Her friend Cassie had asked Raz to go with her to the camp to bring food. On one of her earlier visits, she had organized a few supplies on the one side of the room for easier access.

Walking softly across the room, she stopped next to the man who lay in the cot near the back wall.

His auburn curls lay damp on his forehead and his head turned back and forth in his feverish state.

Moisture beaded his skin and trickled down to his neck.

With a gentle movement of her hand she pushed back the wavy auburn hair that was similar to her own. With the inside of her wrist she touched the sick man's fore-head. "He's still too hot."

She dipped a clean cloth into the cold water she kept nearby. As she placed the cool cloth on his forehead she thought of the many times she had helped her Mother to heal during one of her severe headache episodes.

All those years of learning about different herbal remedies and even some nursing courses online with her Mother was now being put to good use. She was grateful to be able to help in some small way.

Feet shuffled behind her and she turned.

"That's my brother." Hudson whispered as he crept closer to the bed and laid his hand on top of Waylon's.

Raz was touched by the care he showed for his brother. "What's his name?"

"Waylon. He's my younger brother."

Razelle absorbed this information and sighed. "I was afraid of that." She hadn't wanted the sick man to be Hudson's brother. A chill spread up her spine at the thought of them staying at the camp.

"What's wrong with him?"

"It might just be a bad case of the flu, but I'm not sure." Raz cooled his forehead. "What your brother really needs to do is go to the hospital. But sometimes it can be diffi-cult to convince Sloane to let people leave the camp once they are here."

"Who is Sloane?" Luke questioned, a furrow forming between his brows as he stepped closer to the bed.

"He's the leader of this camp. Everybody does what Sloane says, or lives to regret it." Raz spoke in hushed whispers as she mixed some herbs together to help calm Hudson's brother and help him sleep.

"Well Sloane's just going to have to accept it. We're taking him to the hospital." Luke stated in a no-nonsense tone that brooked no argument.

Raz just shrugged and nodded. "It would be for the best." Her experience with Sloane told her they better hurry. "But, if you're going to take him, you should go now before the whole camp wakes up and Sloane and his thugs are alerted to the fact that you're here."

Luke started forward. "Let's do it then. The sooner we leave, the better."

Razelle wrapped the shivering man in more blankets.

Cassie opened the door and Abby stood by her side.

Luke and Hudson carried Waylon through the door.

They had just begun to step past the trees when suddenly a voice boomed out, breaking the silence of the morning.

"Who are you and where do you think you're going with that man?" Sloane's rough voice called out. Razelle could see him limping through the trees. His two body-guards were at his side until he finally came to a stop. They stood in front of Luke and Hudson, blocking their path.

Sweat glistened on Sloane's forehead and his face was as red as the glow from the rising sun behind him.

Luke replied with an even tone. "This man is his brother." He nodded at Hudson. "We're taking him to the hospital so the doctors can figure out what's wrong with him."

Sloane's eyes narrowed at Luke and he nodded at the

men who stood beside him. "No. I'm afraid I can't let you do that."

Luke took a step forward, but Sloane's men raised rifles they carried at their side and aimed them at Luke and Hudson.

Razelle gasped. What was Sloane doing? He was taking his protectiveness over the people at the camp much too far.

"You're seriously going to stop us from getting this man the help he needs?" Luke shook his head and Raz could see a tick forming along his jawline.

"Yes. You're on my turf now and what I say goes."

"But my brother is really sick and needs…" Hudson's brows puckered in worry and was about to say more when Sloane interrupted.

Raz could see the vein in Sloane's neck throbbing and his face twisted in it's angry state.

"No your brother will stay here, like I said."

She needed to do something to stop this situation from getting out of hand.

Razelle spoke up from her place by the doorway. She began walking down the steps. "Sloane, this man is really sick. I don't know what else I can do to help him. Can't you see he needs to be in a hospital?"

"All I see is that you and these two strangers are trying to carry this man - my guest - away sudden-like. And without my say-so." Sloane crossed his arms over his chest, his stance defensive and determined.

"Do you want him to die? That might happen you know. You want that on your conscience?" Raz knew she was pushing any goodwill she might have had with Sloane for fixing his leg a month ago, but she needed to try to talk some sense into him.

Sloane shrugged. "He won't die. Because you all will stay here and take care of him."

Raz expelled a frustrated sigh. "You know I can't stay. My mother expects me home this morning to help her with the cafe."

He nodded to his men to stay where they were and Sloane began walking toward her. He looked at her and then switched his gaze and took a long look at Addy. Walking toward the teenager he pulled her close to his side.

Addy tried to step away, but Sloane wouldn't let her escape.

"Well then Raz, you can go home but everyone else stays." Sloane looked down at Addy before looking up at Razelle a menacing smile on his face. "Besides, I have the perfect insurance to make sure you come back."

Sloane looked down at Addy who was pressed against his side. "I'll keep her nice and safe in the cabin to make sure you come back."

Addy's brown eyes grew large with fear and her face white with tension.

Razelle stepped closer to him. Maybe she could talk some reason into him.

"Sloane, You don't have to do this. I promise, I will be back tomorrow night." She was worried for Addy. The cabin was a small run-down building where Sloane kept people at the camp, who he wanted locked away in isolation. She was scared Addy would go out of her mind there.

"Yes, you will come back tomorrow night." There was steel in Sloane's eyes and a determination in his tone, but Razelle was sure she glimpsed fear in his eyes.

For a moment, she wondered if there was more that the camp leader was hiding. Something or someone that he was afraid of?

Without warning another crack of thunder opened up the heavens overhead and rain began to soaked them.

"All of you get inside the cabin." Sloane ordered and his henchmen pointed their rifles at Luke and Hudson, who turned back and carried Hud's brother back into the cabin.

Razelle was about to follow them, when Sloane called out. "Don't you have somewhere you need to be?"

She nodded slowly and looked first at Addy with what she hoped was a hopeful smile. Turning she looked over at the doorway of the cabin. Luke nodded and tossed her a crooked smile.

Razelle hesitated a moment. She had the feeling Luke was trying to help lessen her worry. She gave him a slight smile and nodded before hurrying down the path toward the river.

As she got in her small paddleboat and rowed to the other side of the creek, troubled thoughts followed her. She worried over Addy, who would now be in lock down in that cabin alone. A new wave of guilt washed over her as Raz remembered it was her fault, because she had led Addy into danger with Sloane.

She also worried over Hudson's brother who was very sick. Raz had taught Cassie much of what she learned, but she was concerned that without going to the hospital Waylon might be in trouble.

Luke and Hudson would help, but she was afraid they might try something stupid like leave the camp. That might make things worse for all her friends at the camp.

Raz parked the old rowboat on the creek bank and hurried up the small hill and down the path that led towards home. She prayed that mother would still be sleeping when she got home.

If not, she would be in real trouble.

"RAZELLE, wake up now. You slept in again!" A hand shook her shoulders and her mother's stern voice called her name stirring her out of a deep sleep.

Her brain felt fuzzy.

Opening her eyes wide, Raz panicked at her Mother's angry brown eyes hovering over her. Pushing herself to sit up in bed, Razelle rubbed her eyes, quickly reaching out toward her nightstand to turn her alarm off.

Her mother stood beside her bed, her arms crossed in front of her chest and a thin line around her mouth.

Razelle knew she was angry. "Sorry Mother. I'll do my best not to sleep in again."

"This is the second time in a month, Razelle. If you've been staying up late reading again, you need to stop. I have enough to do, without needing to get you up in the morning." Her mother looked around the small bedroom, before her gaze fell back to her daughter. "Now hurry and get dressed. I need you to get started before our regulars show up."

"Of course, Mother. I'll be downstairs right away." Razelle expelled a slow breath as her Mother left her bedroom. She got out of her narrow bed and cringed when her feet landed on the cold tile floor. She hurried to her tiny closet and pulled on her grey work shirt.

Her mother told her the first time they moved to Paradise Lake when she was seven, that she planned to save enough money so they would have a place of their own. They had lived in a few of the small towns in this state for years before finally moving back and settling in Paradise Lake.

Razelle had been happy that they settled here. She had been lucky that her mother allowed her to stay friends with Rory and Cassie the whole time they moved from place to place. But Raz longed for a permanent home where they didn't pack up and move all the time.

And she especially liked being back in this small town, living near her friends.

She didn't mind working in the coffee shop with her Mother, but longed for more freedom.

When she was small they lived in Moorea Island. Razelle had spoken mostly in French and had needed to switch to English when they moved back to Washington State.

Her Mother told her when she was a baby they lived in Texas. But her mother insisted that it was a backwoods town and they needed to move. So they moved across the ocean to the French Polynesian Islands.

When they moved back to the States, it had taken Raz

a few months before she was comfortable speaking English once again.

She'd been happy to make new friends here in Paradise Lake.

Rory and Cassie were the kind of friends that were always there for her. She would do anything to help them too. She adored her friends.

Which is why she worried about Cassie and Addy being at the camp.

Slipping on her black work jeans and matching black shoes, she went to her narrow dresser. She brushed back long wavy hair that fell to her knees until it was free of knots. Quickly she made two braids and wrapped them around her head in a crown.

Taking one last look in the small cracked mirror on her dresser, she saw the dark circles under her eyes and hoped that Mother wouldn't be looking too closely at her face today. Raz didn't want her to find out she had disobeyed the rules.

After feeding their fuzzy cat, Raz opened the door of their apartment and hurried down the back stairs that led to the coffee shop. It was early morning, so no customers were there yet.

Their short order cook Miguel, was already mixing the pancake batter. Their coffee shop also served simple breakfast foods and lunch and supper meals so he was here early everyday. They had another cook that took over the afternoon shift.

"Hey Miguel." Raz pulled her apron from the peg behind the door and tired it around her waist. "You're here early."

"Yep. Didn't sleep so good last night. I wanted to get an early start today." He turned to her, a pucker forming between his brows. "You look very tired yourself, little one. You are not sleeping well either?"

"I guess you could say that. Maybe I can catch a few winks during my lunch break." Raz tossed him a half-grin.

"Maybe. But most likely your Mother will ask you to do something else during your lunch time." Miguel stirred the batter, his gaze steady on hers.

Razelle expelled a long breath. "Sadly, I'm sure you're right." Miguel knew how her mother worked and it was true, she was always asking Raz to do something. There was hardly any time she could call her own. "Well, I'll need to try and get the sleep I need tonight then."

"Uh…huh." Miguel shook his head at her in doubt.

Razelle sighed, realizing that she wouldn't be able to catch up on sleep tonight either. She was needed at the camp.

Taking out the coffee grounds she went to the different coffee makers they had lined up behind the counter. She filled each with water and then added the coffee grounds and turned on each machine. Grabbing the bowls of coffee flavourings and toppings out of the fridge, she placed them beside the coffee carafe on the counter.

Checking the time she realized that she had only a few minutes before their regular customers showed up.

Raz added the batter to the mixing bowl and started the muffins just as her Mother walked in. "Razelle, you need to wipe down the tables again. There are streaks. After you have the muffins in the oven, I'd like you to get started on that."

"Of course, Mother." Raz looked up at her and forced a smile to hide any disappointment. Her mother never seemed to appreciate anything she did. Somehow whatever she did was never good enough.

"See that you do." Mother left the kitchen to serve the first customers that came in the early morning.

Amid the smell of coffee and the chatter of people, Raz finished baking the first batch of muffins. She put them on the counter where they displayed the fresh baked goods.

By mid-morning she had made three batches of muffins, banana bread and had cleaned the counters and tables and was ready for her coffee break. Her mother was busy talking with customers when it was time for her break, so Razelle went to sit outside to rest for a moment.

Their small town street was busy with neighbors calling out to each other in greeting and townspeople walking down the sidewalks. It was a sunny day and Raz loved to watch the people.

She saw a woman walking beside her husband. The man held a toddler in one arm and had his other arm around his wife. The way the man looked at the woman was filled with so much love. They were laughing, smiling and enjoying life together.

Razelle yearned to be part of a loving family.

She was so weary of working in the coffee shop and only getting away from their little apartment when Mother gave her permission.

Cassie thought her mother had too much control over her life. She agreed, but didn't know if she had courage to leave.

So for now, she would stay with her Mother. Maybe someday she would go out on her own.

And tonight, she would be back at the camp. She hoped Addy, Cassie, Luke, Hudson and his brother were all okay. She intended to do everything she could so they were safe.

Together they would figure out a way to get away from Sloane without getting hurt.

Maybe they could put their heads together and figure out a plan tonight.

CHAPTER FOUR

uke

"HOW IS WAYLON FEELING?" Razelle whispered softly, her brows puckered in worry as she entered the cabin late that night.

With shaky hands she pushed wet hair from her face.

Loud cracks of thunder shook the cabin.

Luke didn't want to admit it even to himself, but he'd been waiting for her. All day long his thoughts had been on the auburn haired beauty. He was attracted to her. He knew it and was doing his best to fight against it.

He'd even tried to discover flaws about her today. When he'd asked Cassie about her friend, she told Luke that Razelle was kind and generous and the best friend she'd ever had.

When Luke had asked Cassie why her friend seemed

anxious to return back home, Cassie had only said her Mother had strict rules. She told him if he wanted to know more, he'd need to ask Raz.

She seemed too good to be true, which in his experience meant it usually was.

Problem was, now he was more determined than ever to get to know her better.

Walking to the door, Luke helped take the backpack off her shoulders. Using his thumb he wiped moisture from her face. For a moment, Raz's gaze met his.

Luke's hand lingered along her jawline a moment longer than necessary.

Green eyes met his, hesitant and uncertain.

"I'm glad you're back." He whispered for her ears only. A tell-tale blush blossomed in her cheeks. His eyes swept down her face, from Raz's eyes to her lips, the urge to kiss her almost overpowering.

Razelle wiped away moisture that continued to drip from her wet hair.

"I'm glad to be back." She reached out and placed a trembling hand on her backpack. Luke reluctantly let go. She looked over at Waylon who lay in the cot at the far end of the cabin. "How is he?"

Luke was glad she switched the topic of conversation. He needed somewhere else to focus his wayward thoughts. "The fever has lessened somewhat, but now he's developed a deep chest cough."

"Hmmm, not good." All of a sudden her attention switched to the sick man and she hurried over to Waylon's bedside.

Luke followed and watched as she took charge of the situation.

Waylon was waking up. He stared at Razelle, confusion in his eyes. "Who are you?"

"I'm Razelle."

He tried to sit up.

"Just rest okay?" Razelle spoke softly. She placed a cool cloth on his head as she spoke.

Waylon lay his head back down on the pillow, exhausted.

His brother Hudson, moved a chair next to his bed. "Hey man. How are you feeling?"

"Not so good." He shivered. Razelle covered him with another blanket.

"We need to get you out of here and to a hospital. If I could, I'd call the ambulance to get you, but I don't have access to cell phone reception here at the camp. We'll need to leave soon." Luke stared at Waylon, worried as his friend lay there shivering and coughing.

"Luke just take me home." A sudden coughing fit overtook Waylon for a few minutes until it finally stopped. His sick friend lay back on the bed, weakened and drained of energy.

"We will." Luke stood beside him and reached out squeezing his hand for a moment. "Don't worry, we'll get you better."

Luke looked around at Hudson, Razelle and Cassie who all seemed to be looking to him for direction.

"We'll need to pack up supplies we need. Then keep a lookout for when the guards step away from the cabin, because that'll be our only chance to get away from here." Luke looked around to see them all nodding.

"I'll gather my things." Razelle hesitated before she whispered. "What should we do about Addy? She is stuck in that cabin all alone and she's not safe from Sloane. We should take her with us."

Razelle twirled tendrils of wavy auburn hair that slipped out of the braid. He recalled that Raz twirled her hair when she was anxious or worried about something.

Luke nodded.

It was the right thing to do. But, he wasn't looking forward to figuring out a way to get past Sloane's guards.

"I'll do my best to try to bring her with us." A sigh of relief escaped Razelle's lips and Luke straightened his shoulders.

He couldn't help it, he liked the fact that she needed him.

Cassie followed Razelle to clean up and gather their things.

Hudson walked over to the window and peered behind the thick curtain. "There's one guard still out there, but he's looking a little uncomfortable with all the rain. Maybe he'll take shelter somewhere soon."

Luke was surprised that they were still out there in this weather. "We'll keep checking. When it's all clear we'll head out."

Razelle spoke softly. "We'll need to do our best to keep most of the rain from soaking Waylon."

Hudson pulled off his hoodie. "My brother can wear my hoodie. I'll be fine."

"That would be helpful." Razelle adjusted her backpack

and helped Cassie adjust the straps on her backpack too. "As soon as it's all clear, we're ready to go."

Luke nodded and checked his watch. It was now three in the morning. It was getting late. They needed to leave soon.

Hudson walked over to the window. "I can't see the guards anywhere. Its still pouring rain, but this might be a good time to leave."

"Good." Luke walked over to help Hudson get Waylon to his feet. He was unsteady, but they managed to hold him up on either side. He nodded at Razelle who stood by the door. "Let's get out of here."

She opened the door and Luke and Hudson walked as fast as they could with Waylon between them. Luke could hear Razelle and Cassie coming up behind them and she hurried in front of them to lead the way to the creek.

"It's not much farther." She whispered and motioned for them to follow.

Before long they arrived at the rowboat. Luke and Hudson helped Waylon to sit inside and then he turned to the group. "I'm going back for Addy. Maybe you should all head out now. I'll be along shortly."

Hudson shook his head.

Razelle spoke up. "No. We'll wait for you."

Luke nodded and couldn't help but admire her loyalty.

Turning, he ran back through the trees and back up the embankment to the camp. Hiding behind trees and cabins that were scattered throughout the area, he ran until the ramshackle cabin came into view.

He waited a few moments and watched to see if guards were posted outside.

When he didn't see anyone, Luke ran toward the cabin and was nearing the building, when the cabin door opened and Sloane stepped outside. Seeing Luke, Sloane reached for the shotgun that rested against the cabin wall.

Luke ran, weaving between trees and buildings. Shots fired all around him, spurring him to run faster.

"You won't get far. I'll track you down." Sloane yelled from behind him. Luke looked behind, and saw his nemesis trying to catch up with him, but Sloane's gimped leg slowed him down.

Luke continued to run, zigzagging his way behind trees as he made his way back to the boat. He realized he would need to try again another time to get Addy out of there.

Without warning, searing pain hit his leg. Blood rushed away from his face, and his body trembled.

He glanced down at his blood-soaked jeans and realized he'd been shot.

Limping forward he nearly fell down, but managed to keep going.

The others waited for him. Pushing himself, Luke finally made it to the rowboat.

He hobbled inside. "Let's get going. We're being followed."

Hudson started rowing away quickly and Luke grabbed the other set of oars.

"Where's Addy?" Razelle questioned, fear in her eyes.

"I couldn't get to her. Sloane was guarding the place." Luke shook his head with regret. "We'll go back for her later."

Razelle inhaled sharply, nodding slowly her brows puckered in worry.

They were almost to the other side of the creek when Luke spotted someone running down the creek bank on the other side.

"It's difficult to see in the dark, but I think Sloane is on the other side trying to figure out how he can stop us."

Razelle spoke suddenly. "Sloane won't cross the river. He might take the road and cross the river that way, but he won't get in a boat or swim to cross it."

"How can you be so sure?" Luke questioned as he paddled harder to reach the shore.

"Because everyone in the camp knows that Sloane's grandmother told him when he was a child that his death lay in the river. He won't cross. He's more fearful of that than anything else." Her confident tone convinced him of the truth of her words.

They got out of the boat and Luke held his aching leg as they hurried behind some trees.

There were a few gunshots still being fired across the river. A couple of them hit a few trees. It was better to stay out of their way.

As happy as Luke was that Sloane wouldn't cross the river, it didn't mean that at some point the man wouldn't try to get his revenge.

But Luke didn't want to think of that now. For the moment, he just wanted to get Waylon to the hospital.

Moaning, Luke leaned for a moment against a large tree.

"LUKE, WHAT'S WRONG?" Razelle ran toward him. His head rested against the tree while one hand held his leg. The rain had slowed down until there was only a light misty spray in the air.

She looked down and gasped when she saw the blood. "What happened?"

"Sloane got me, but I think it's only a graze. He's a better shot than I thought." Luke's crooked smile was endearing and he looked calm, but the pain in his eyes convinced her otherwise.

"Mind if I take a look?" Razelle knelt on the wet ground and looked up at him, waiting for permission.

He waved his hand and said. "Be my guest."

She gently looked at the tear in his pants just above the knee. The area was covered in blood.

She tore open the ripped fabric a little further so she could see the area closely.

Opening her backpack she pulled out clean rags and gently wiped at the wound. It was a long red gash that had furrowed a few several layers of skin.

It looked like a giant skid mark on his thigh. "You're right, it looks like the bullet grazed your leg. But the skin is pierced and red. We'll need to get antiseptic and maybe some stitches. The doctor at the Hospital can take care of you."

Hudson walked up to them, with one arm around Waylon to hold him steady. "I was able to get a call through to my brother Sawyer. He'll pick us up at the top of the ridge."

"That's good. I'll help you up the hill." Razelle put his arm around her shoulder and she placed her other arm around his waist. They started walking and soon Cassie planted herself on Luke's other side.

As soon as they reached the top of the hill a large SUV stood waiting for them. Razelle watched as a tall man with reddish brown hair so similar to his two brothers walked towards Waylon and Hudson.

"You look done in, Waylon." Sawyer opened the truck door before he turned to the three of them.

Walking toward Luke, he shook his head. "What happened to you, Luke?"

"Dodged a bullet. I'll be fine."

"We'll need to get you to the hospital along with Waylon."

"Uh, about that Sawyer." Hudson began. "I was thinking maybe mom should fix up Luke, after all she is a nurse. If the Doc at the hospital sees Luke with a bullet wound, they might want to know what happened and then they'll get the police involved. Then, Waylon would be questioned by the police, and let's just say that isn't a good idea."

Sawyer shook his head. "What did Waylon do this time?"

"Stole a motorbike." Waylon's hoarse voice could be heard inside the SUV as they walked closer.

"Okay, no hospital and no police." Sawyer sighed. "But you know what Dad will say."

"I know, I know." Waylon rubbed his head with a shaky hand. "I will return the motorbike and make amends." He leaned his head back against the back seat.

Hudson spoke up in a no-nonsense tone of voice. "And you've got to promise to stay away from that camp."

"I will, I promise."

Luke turned to Waylon and spoke in low tones. "It seems you go a little crazy every year at the start of summer."

"I know. I don't know why." There was a heaviness in Waylon's voice, that concerned Luke.

Luke studied his friend. "I can guess." He paused for a moment before he continued. "You miss your sister. I get it, I really do. Some days I miss my dad so much it hurts. But, you can't bring her back, Waylon. And doing crazy stunts like this is going to hurt you — not to mention hurting your dad and mom."

Waylon expelled a breath. "I know. I'll stop, I promise." His brows puckered together and he bit his bottom lip before he whispered. "Can we go home now, please?" He shivered from the front seat and leaned his head back, closing his eyes.

Razelle took a light blanket that she carried in her backpack and wrapped it around him.

Both her and Cassie helped Luke get inside the truck. He moaned in pain as he sat down on the seat. Razelle shifted in the seat beside him, trying to help him get comfortable.

Luke turned to her, his forehead thick with perspiration. "Thank you for your help today."

Razelle nodded, reaching over and giving his hand a light squeeze. "You're welcome." She removed her hand quickly, embarrassed that she so easily shared her thoughts and feelings with this man.

This was Luke Stevenson, for heaven's sake. What was she thinking?

Tingles skittered up her arm where his skin touched hers.

Sitting so close to this man — even now when he wasn't feeling good — drove her a little crazy. She was drawn to him in a way she didn't understand.

Luke was handsome, but also kind and compassionate.

He'd proved it by trying to go back to get her friend Addy. To make matters worse, it was her fault that Luke got shot.

If she hadn't asked him to go back for her friend, he wouldn't have been hurt.

She shifted her body a little so she wasn't touching him and was relieved when the truck arrived on the Donovan family ranch.

A woman walked out of the house to meet them as they got out of the truck. She had dark red hair streaked with slivers of grey and wore jeans and a plaid shirt. Every inch of her looked like a ranch woman.

"Hey mom." Waylon wrapped his arms around his mother. His mother stifled a small gasp.

"We were so worried about you." A single tear ran down her cheek as she stepped back a little to look at her son's face.

"I'm sorry for disappearing and making you worried. Forgive me?" Waylon looked at his mother and her face lit up.

"You know I do. Always." His mom kissed his cheek and wrapped her arm around his waist and looked over to see everyone.

She stopped for a moment and stared when she saw Razelle.

Mrs. Donovan looked at her for the longest time, her eyes lingering on her face.

"Mom, this is Razelle." Hudson broke the silence. "This is her friend Cassie and of course you know Luke." Hudson introduced everyone and finally his mom's gaze shifted to include everyone.

"Yes, of course." She waved her arm to indicate they should follow. She walked next to Waylon into the house. "Let's get you all cleaned up and on the mend."

Razelle, looked around their large ranch house. The open space between the large kitchen, dining room and great room was so welcoming. This place felt so much like home, she fell in love with it immediately.

Mrs. Donovan spoke to Luke. "I want to take a look at your leg, but I'll need you to get cleaned up first to do it." She looked over at her son. "Hudson lend Luke a pair of your short pants will you? That way I'll be able to see what we're looking at."

She got her first aid supplies and set them on the kitchen table.

"Can I do something to help?" Razelle followed her to where she sat sorting through things. Cassie came to sit at the table with them.

"Oh no, I think I have everything I need right here." Mrs. Donovan looked over at her, with that curious look in her green eyes. But at that moment, Luke walked into the room, before Razelle could summon up the courage to speak.

"I'm ready." Luke limped toward the table. He wore short pants and Razelle couldn't help but admire the muscles in his long legs. He was a handsome man in every way.

But she needed to stop thinking about Luke and her attraction to him. Being interested in him would lead to nothing. Any relationship with him would never work.

Her Mother had made it clear that there were to be no men in her life right now. Mother told Razelle she needed her daughter too much right now, for her to be running around with a man.

Razelle didn't understand her Mother sometimes.

As Luke neared she got a closer look at his leg. The wound was an angry red gash down his thigh.

She winced, wondering how much pain he felt.

Looking into Luke's eyes, he winked at her just before he sat down at the kitchen table. Heat crept up to her cheeks. *He was too sure of himself by far.* Her jaw dropped slightly as he tossed her a rogue smile.

Razelle wasn't sure what to think, not really. She liked it when Luke flirted with her, but it didn't feel right to encourage him when she knew that their relationship couldn't go anywhere.

She looked down at her hands, anything to avoid meeting Luke's gaze.

"There now, you're all cleaned up Luke. It'll take a few weeks to really heal though." Mrs. Donovan cleaned up the first aid kit just as Hudson and Sawyer walked into the room.

Razelle gaze caught the morning sunrise coming through the kitchen window, and looked at the clock. It was almost six. Her mother would be awake any moment.

"I — er Cassie and I need to get home." Razelle looked at her friend who stood beside her.

"I'll drive you back home." Hudson offered.

Razelle nodded. "Thank you. We'd appreciate that." She turned to Mrs. Donovan. "Thank you for having us in your home for a short time. I'm glad your son is home now."

"My dear, Waylon told me how you took care of him. Thanks for doing that for my boy and for bringing him home. And please know that you're welcome to come back anytime." Mrs. Donovan's warm voice and the loving look in her eyes brought a sudden prick of moisture to Raz's eyes.

"Thank you." Raz quickly nodded and turned to smile at everyone else in the room before she hurried to the porch. Cassie followed close behind, slipping her shoes on.

She bit her lip to keep from melting into a puddle of tears.

Mrs. Donovan's heartfelt words had touched her to the core. In her heart, she felt like she was leaving something important behind as she got up to leave. This home was filled with so much love and acceptance.

Razelle desperately wished she could trade in her ordinary life of loneliness and insecurity for a life of acceptance and love.

Shoving her shoulders back, she sighed. That was not to be. And the sooner she accepted that, the better off she'd be.

She whispered to her friend. "We need to hurry."

"I know. I think Hudson knows too, because he's already waiting by the door." Cassie whispered.

Razelle stood to her feet and looked around for her backpack.

Suddenly a warm hand squeezed hers. In the other hand Luke held her backpack. "I'll walk you outside." He whispered in her ear.

Startled, she could only nod. She waved goodbye to everyone else and followed Hudson and Cassie to the truck.

Luke walked by her side. "I know you need to get home. But, I want to see you again. Can I pick you up on Saturday? I'll take you to a favorite restaurant of mine."

"I can't, Luke." Razelle looked at him and shook her head. She wished she could say yes, but there was no way this relationship would work.

Luke didn't give up. "Okay, not Saturday then. How about Sunday or sometime next week?"

Razelle sighed and looked him in the eye. "You don't understand, Luke. I can't go out with you at all."

"What? Give me one good reason." He touched her shoulder to stop her from getting in the truck. His serious look held her in place.

"I just can't. You'll just have to accept that." Razelle shook her head and looked at her shoes for a moment. She didn't want to tell Luke all the sordid details of life or about her overprotective and controlling Mother.

She would rather just let him think that she was turning him down.

"Razelle, what's going on?" Luke gently moved his

hand under her chin, lifting her head. His brown eyes were filled with concern and compassion.

"I can't tell you that. Please, Luke I have to go." Pinpricks of tears began behind her eyes. She held out her hand for him to give her the back pack.

Luke's hand brushed hers in a gentle caress as he gave it to her and she quickly lowered her head and stepped past him, getting into the truck.

He leaned over and whispered. "This isn't over, not by a long shot."

Luke closed the truck door and Razelle looked out her window and watched as he got smaller and smaller in the window until he faded from sight.

She told herself to keep that picture vivid in her mind. Because that was exactly how the memory of Luke needed to disappear from her heart.

The sun was beginning to rise when Hudson's truck reached the street that led to her home.

"Just drop me off a block from home. I'll walk the rest of the way. Thanks Hudson." Razelle got out of the truck.

Cassie leaned over and whispered. "If there's trouble, leave a note for me by the tree."

Razelle nodded.

Fear coiled in the pit of her stomach as she hurried down the back alley, letting herself into their backyard through the hole in the wood fence.

She climbed the tree and reaching the window to her bedroom, silently slipped inside.

"Well, look who finally decided to come home?" Mother's syrupy sweet voice greeted her as her shoes feet landed on the floor inside the bedroom.

Razelle began to brace herself for the worst. "I'm sorry Mother."

"Where have you been? I woke up an hour ago and came to your bedroom only to find my daughter was gone. I was worried sick."

"I was at the camp down by the river."

"Why on earth would you go to a horrible place like that?" Mother stood in front of her hands on her hips, her face red with anger. The vein was beginning to pulse in her neck, which meant she was very angry.

"Sometimes I help people get better with my herbs. Other times I bring a little food for people who don't have any." Without warning, the palm of her Mother's hand hit her cheek forcibly.

The sting of pain and the force behind the blow caused her to step back.

"You dare take food out of my cafe, to feed homeless people? They are getting what they deserve." Her Mother's comment horrified Razelle.

"Mother that's not true…"

Her mother walked closer to her, the vein in her neck pulsating with the staccato rhythm of her words. "Quiet! You. Listen. To. Me. You're a liar, a thief and since you've been at that camp, you're most likely a hussy too."

Razelle could feel the blood drain out of her face at her mother's harsh words. She wanted to deny her accusations, but knew it wouldn't do her any good.

"I don't ever want you to bring food from my coffee shop to that camp again, do you understand?"

Mother waited until Raz nodded before she continued. "And that's not all. I don't want you to go there ever again.

And to ensure that you don't, I'm going to keep you in lock down here for at least six months until you come to your senses. You are grounded."

"I'm sorry." Razelle's body trembled visibly at the thought of being isolated once again.

"You should've thought of that before. Now it's too late." Her mother held out her hand. "Hand over your phone."

Razelle reached into her backpack and dropped her cell phone into her mother's open hand.

Her phone was the only source of communication she had with her friends. Now — for at least for six months — all she would have is her mother and her friend Miguel to talk to.

"Except for your work in the coffee shop, you are grounded to this apartment. No going anywhere else. Do you understand?" Mother's words rang in her ears like a death knell.

"Yes Mother." Razelle nodded, but suddenly felt like she could hardly breathe.

As her mother walked away, Raz wondered how she would survive six months of not talking to any of her friends or seeing anyone who really cared about her.

It seemed all her mother cared about was making sure her daughter followed her rules. There was no laughter and no fun.

Mother accused her often enough of being ugly. Telling her, she was a hussy who no decent man would ever want to date.

Her words had cut deep, like they did again tonight. Were those words true about her?

A happy memory came back from when she saw Mrs. Donovan today. She was loving and accepting of her sons and she was kind even to strangers. That was the kind of Mother and the type of family that Razelle had dreamed of being part of.

Why was her own mother so mean and strict with her? Did she hate her?

Tears flowed down her cheeks.

She had very real doubts that her mother would ever allow her to fall in love and marry.

Was there any way that she could do what her friends Cassie and Rory suggested?

Could she leave her Mother?

uke

A TRILL of laughter greeted Luke as he got out of his truck and hurried up the front stairs of his mom's new beach-front house.

He was glad to get together with his family today.

For the last five days, all he'd thought of was Razelle. He missed her and was worried about her.

When he'd last seen her at Donovan's ranch, she had told him a firm no to them dating. But, he was convinced he'd detected fear in her eyes that day.

What was she afraid of?

He'd tried texting her cell phone, but got no answer.

His next step was to stop by the cafe. He had to see her.

But, he wasn't able to talk to her there either.

Today, he was happy to spend time with his family, but he would try again to get in touch with Razelle.

Two months ago Eliza Stevenson had sold her old house, in favor of a beach house along the lake in their small town.

She had told each of her sons that she wanted to be closer to their families so she could get to know her grandchildren better.

Even though Luke missed the old house, he was glad his mom now lived nearby.

Just as he reached the front door, it opened quickly.

"Luke you're here. Your mother will be so happy to see you." Therese greeted him and opened the door wide. Her brown eyes sparkled and her smile grew big.

Therese had been Eliza's cook and companion for years now. All his brothers had got together to pay for someone to be with their mom and cook for her.

His mom didn't think it was a good idea at the time, but now mom admitted, she wouldn't know how to get everything done without Therese.

Luke kissed her cheek. "Hi Therese. I can smell the barbecue cooking already. You are a wonder."

"Aww, thank you Luke. But I know what you really want. You want me to save the best pieces of barbecue for you."

He chuckled. "You have me figured out. Is it working?"

"Maybe." Therese grinned as she led the way to the French doors that opened up onto the large back deck.

She waved at the family who was on the beach. "Everyone, Luke's here." Therese announced his name and his younger brother Zach, his older brothers and their wives turned to greet him.

Luke hurried down the stairs from the deck and out onto the sandy beach.

His mom stood to her feet from her comfy beach chair and gave him a big hug. "Ah Luke. It's so good to see you." He wrapped his arms around his mom, showing with his actions what he could never really find the words to say.

"I wouldn't miss a Stevenson family celebration. Happy housewarming, Mom. I love you." Luke leaned down and kissed her cheek.

His mother's smile lit up her whole face and her blue eyes sparkled. "Thank you, Luke. I love you too."

She removed the large beach towel from his shoulder, so she could see his leg. "I know you said Millie Donovan took care of your leg, but I wanted to see for myself." Her brows puckered together in worry.

Luke looked down at the wrinkled red scar that ran down his thigh. "It doesn't look good Mom, but it's not completely healed yet. Just give it time."

His mom straightened her shoulders, worry shimmering in her blue eyes. "Is the matter finished?"

He knew she was asking if he was going to have any more run-ins with the guy who did this to him. "Yes. I certainly don't have any reason to see Sloane again."

"Good." His mom let out a sigh of relief.

Luke put a comforting arm around her shoulders. "I'm fine mom."

"I know you are. And I'm thankful for that." Eliza Stevenson straightened her shoulders, smiling up at him once more. "Well then, let's enjoy this afternoon together."

His brothers and their wives were soaking up the sun. Luke waked toward them.

"I see Zach's entertaining Daniel, Walker and little Delanie." Luke grinned as he watched his younger brother build sand castles with the toddlers. "It looks like they are showing him how it's done."

The little ones were busy molding and shaping the sand into shapes that made a crooked looking sandcastle. Between the tickling and the giggles they were having a lot of fun.

"Yep. It's been nice to have our own built in babysitter." Jack grinned looking at Bella who was pregnant with their second child.

"Just wait until you have baby number two, Jack. Suddenly you'll be busier than ever and find that you need that built in babysitter more than you ever did." Adam grinned and looked adoringly at the new baby daughter he held in his arms.

Elle smiled and adjusted the baby's blanket around their little daughter. "It's true. We're busier now, but our little Katie makes it all worthwhile."

"It won't be long before Gabe and Rory have a new little one. Do you know if you're having a boy or girl?" Elle asked Rory, who had a smaller baby bump than Bella.

"We wanted to be surprised." Rory grinned. "But my three aunts are chomping at the bit, because they really want to know. They already spoil little Delanie, so it'll be really fun for them and for us when this new little one is born." Rory rubbed her pregnant belly lightly and smiled.

Luke watched his brothers with their wives, enjoying the back and forth banter. Somewhere deep inside a desire was sparked. He wanted that loving banter with his wife.

He wanted children to play with.

He wanted a family of his own to love.

Razelle's beautiful face lingered in his mind.

Luke pushed thoughts of love aside.

He still didn't believe in love.

But, Luke really wanted that land and he'd only get it if he married.

Maybe there was a way he could have what he wanted, after all.

He desperately needed to talk to one of his brothers and hear their much needed advice.

It wasn't long before they all headed to the barbecue, enjoying Therese's delicious food.

When they finished eating, Therese carried a beautiful cake to the table.

Luke spoke up. "Happy housewarming Mom."

"Hear, hear." Gabe spoke up and everyone around the time chimed in with congratulations.

Eliza Stevenson looked around at each of her sons, their wives and her grandchildren, a contented smile on her face. "You all have made me so happy today, just by being here. I'm grateful for each of you."

"Ah, Mom. We're thankful to have you nearby." Luke spoke softly, squeezing his mom's arm.

Moisture filled Eliza's eyes as she reached over and squeezed his hand. "I know I'll love it. More time with the grandchildren."

Soon the grandchildren were busy eating cake with the help of their parents.

It didn't take long before the little ones were tuckered out.

After the grandchildren fell asleep they were tucked into their toddler beds that Grandma had added to two rooms in the house. Therese offered to listen for when they woke up.

The adults sat on the deck, sipping their iced tea and enjoying the view of the orange-red glow of the sunset shining a narrow path across the lake.

Restless, Luke carried his drink to the edge of the deck, his gaze taking in the swirl of colors reflected on the water.

It wasn't long before all four of his brothers joined him there.

Jack bumped his shoulder. "How have things been going at Grand's old cabin?"

"Good. I've renovated the inside and almost finished the outside deck. It's been a big project. But you know all about handling big projects." Luke was reminded of Jack's creative design business and his most recent project of the Adventure Park just outside of Paradise Lake.

"Yeah, I do. But you did this by yourself without hiring out. Dad would be proud."

"It's true." Adam spoke up. "But I'm curious what you're going to do about keeping that cabin and the land."

"Yeah, big brother. Have you found a wife to marry yet?" Zach spoke up a teasing grin on his face.

The corners of Luke's lips turned up and he stood for a moment not saying anything. "Maybe."

"You know Luke, your one-word answers are going to be the death of us all." Gabe, the talkative one of the bunch teased him. "Exactly what do you mean maybe? Does this mean you've found a woman you love and want to marry?"

Luke expelled a breath. He couldn't help it that he was the quiet one. He always had been. But, he supposed he should explain himself better. "Not love. But someone I could possibly marry."

"Well, it's a start. Remember, each of us began our relationships with a marriage of convenience." Jack looked at Adam and Gabe as he spoke.

"Yeah I know. Problem is, she's refusing to go on a date with me so we can talk." Luke looked at each of his older brothers, and shrugged.

"Did she say why?"

"Just that she can't talk about it and that I'd be better off forgetting about her." Luke ran a hand through his hair, his emotions all in a tangle every time he thought about Razelle.

"Hmm. Maybe you need to go cave-man on her." At Jack's suggestion, all his brothers laughed.

"What exactly do you mean by that?" Shaking his head, he looked at Jack expectantly.

Jack grinned. "You go to her house. Get her attention somehow and convince her to marry you."

"I might get in trouble with her Mother. I've been told she's very strict and controlling." Luke shook his head.

"So? Get creative." Jack insisted. "Does she have a window to her bedroom? Leave a note or serenade her. Do something to get her attention without her Mother finding out."

"That might work." The more Luke thought of that

idea, the more he liked it. "You've given me something to think about."

"Well, you do want your inheritance from Grand right?"

Luke nodded.

"Sometimes to get what you really want, you have to be persistent and creative." Jack nudged his shoulder. "Whatever you do, don't give up Luke. If you like her, marry her."

"Thanks." Luke nodded and smiled at each of his brothers. "I'll think about it."

As Luke drove back to the cabin he made a decision. Maybe there was something to Jack's advice.

He had no trouble being persistent and creative. He'd done that all his life.

He would do what it took to win her over, even if it meant using cave-man tactics.

&

"Hey, Hud." Luke called his best friend the next day.

"Hi Luke. How are you feeling?"

"Better. You can tell your mom, my leg is healing fine thanks to her."

"I'm glad. Waylon's on the mend too."

"Good." Luke could hear the relief in Hudson's voice.

"What's up?"

"Well, I was wondering if you might have Cassie's phone number or address? I need to talk to her. I need to know how I can reach her friend. Razelle's gone all silent on me, and I don't know how to get in touch."

"Sorry man." Hudson was rustling papers on his side of the phone. "Yes, I do have her cell number." Hudson rambled off the numbers. "You could also stop by the coffee shop and talk to Razelle there."

"I already did." Luke sighed heavily. "Her mother is keeping her in the kitchen and won't even let her come to the front counter."

"That's crazy."

"That's what I thought too. Anyway, I'll see if I can get more answers." Luke sighed. "Thanks man. Talk soon."

Luke ended the call and quickly called Cassie.

There was no time like the present.

"Cassie here."

"Hi Cassie, it's Luke."

"Hey Luke. How's your leg doing?" Cassie sounded surprised to hear from him.

"It's slowly healing."

"Good." Cassie sighed. "Why did you call?"

Luke hesitated. "I wanted to ask you if you've heard from Razelle. I've texted and she hasn't got back to me."

"I haven't heard from her either." Cassie sighed on the other end of the phone line. "Sadly, my guess is that her Mother has taken her phone away and hasn't allowed her contact with anyone."

"What?" Luke was stunned. "Razelle is an adult. That's… that's barbaric. Parents aren't supposed to do that to their adult children."

"Well, Raz's Mother is very strict and controlling… and she's done that and more a few times before."

Luke paced the small cabin and stepped out onto the

deck needing some air. Some kind of protective instinct rose up inside of him.

"Then how am I supposed to talk to her or see her?"

"You could try leaving a note tied to the string that hangs from the tree outside her bedroom window like I do. Or, you could try knocking on her window. But you'd want to do that at midnight or later, so her Mother doesn't hear you." Cassie spoke so matter-of-fact, like this is something she did all the time.

His heart pummelled against his chest. "You're saying this has happened before to Razelle?"

"Oh yes, many times. That's why we have a system figured out."

Luke ran a hand through his hair. "Well, I'll do that then."

"Good. And remember you need to be really quiet. You don't want her Mother to hear you." Cassie said.

After he hung up, Luke stood on his deck, his one hand in a white knuckled grip against the railing.

His mind was racing. He hadn't known how hard it was for Razelle. It was crazy that her Mother locked her up like some kind of dangerous animal.

His thoughts were rattled by what Cassie had told him.

It was pure nonsense, what was going on in Razelle's life.

He needed to help her.

Walking into the cabin, he penned a note.

Tomorrow night I'll be knocking on your window at midnight. We need to talk. L.

Luke waited until it was midnight before he drove to her house. He parked his truck a block away and walked down the back alley and quietly slipped into their backyard. A large oak tree was nestled against the house stretching up to Raz's window.

Looking up, he saw all was dark in all three of the windows that faced the backyard on the second floor. He hoped she would see his note before he came tomorrow night.

He searched for the string and finally found it. He tied the note to a rock, making sure it was tied tight.

As he walked away and drove home, Luke's heartbeat accelerated. He was really looking forward to seeing Razelle again.

§

RAZELLE SLIPPED INTO HER PYJAMAS. It was eleven in the evening and she had just finished helping her mother to fall asleep after one of her bad headaches. She'd given her a large pot of herbal tea that would help her sleep.

She was glad Mother was at long last sound asleep. Whenever her mother was asleep, it felt like she finally had a few hours of freedom.

Although, freedom wasn't something she really had right now.

But, she would make the best of it. Tonight she was happy to finally have a chance to stay awake for a while and read.

Razelle got comfortable on her bed and dived into a favorite novel. Sunbeam lay on her lap, purring loudly. She ran her fingers through her cat's thick fur, as she read.

She got lost in the romance.

All of a sudden a loud scratching sound pierced the stillness.

Setting her book down, she picked up her cat and walked to the window.

As she moved the curtain aside, she gasped and put her hand on her chest.

Luke Stevenson stood outside her window.

Gently she pushed up the window, so she could talk to him.

What are you doing here?" Razelle whispered.

Luke grinned as he sat crouched on the slanted roof outside her window.

"I see you didn't get my note."

"What note?"

"Cassie told me to tie a note to the rope on your tree and you'd get it. But you must have been busy." Luke stared into her eyes as if looking for something.

"Sorry I didn't have time. It's been a very long day." Sunbeam jumped out of her arms, and Raz crossed her arms over her chest. "Why are you here?"

"Cassie also said most likely your Mother took your phone and has stopped you from contacting your friends. Is that true?"

Razelle expelled a long breath. "Cassie talks too much." She made a mental note to tell her friend, not to share so much of her personal life with men she didn't know that well.

"So it's true?"

"Yes, but why should that matter to you?" Razelle didn't want to let down her guard. There was some part of her — deep inside — that somehow knew if she let down the walls around her heart when she was near Luke, it could only end in pain.

Luke cocked his head to the side staring at her silently for a moment. His warm brown eyes, like melted chocolate, affected her deeply — too deeply.

"You know why. I like you Razelle. And I really want to get to know you better."

Razelle giggled softly. "Even knowing all this?" She waved her arm encompassing herself and all her circumstances in that picture.

"Yes. So will you give me a chance?" Luke reached for her hands, holding them between his own.

Warm tingles shot up her arm at his touch. He was too charming by half. Could she do this?

"Sure we can chat now and then. But we need to keep this our secret." Razelle didn't want to experience another one of her mother's outbursts.

"I promise." Heat crept from her neck up to her cheeks at the intensity of Luke's gaze.

"Okay then." Razelle didn't know what in the world she was agreeing to. It was crazy.

She nodded and smiled slightly.

"Good. I'll be back." Luke kissed her hands.

Her hands began to tingle where his warm lips touched her skin. She watched him climb down the tree and didn't close her window until he slipped out of their backyard.

What had she just agreed to do?

Wiping the perspiration from her brow, Razelle hung up the mop.

She surveyed the kitchen floor of the coffee shop, double checked that she'd cleaned every spot. Her mother had been especially tough on her and tonight she'd had to do a thorough cleaning of the fridge, the grill, the pantry and mop the floor.

It was late and she was so very tired.

The creak of the stairway warned Raz that her mother was coming. She'd just tidied up the bucket and put away the wet rags, when her mother showed up in the kitchen doorway.

Her mother's dark brown eyes were cool as she surveyed the work her daughter did that evening.

Razelle really hoped she wouldn't force her to re-do it as she had many times before.

Finally, her mother looked at her and forcibly said. "I'm satisfied for now."

Razelle knew better than to expect any thank you or appreciation for her work. Not once, in all her growing up years, did she remember her mother praising her or thanking her for something she'd done.

She'd learned long ago that it was simply expected of her and she needed to get her work done or there would be trouble.

Nodding, Razelle hung up her apron and headed up the stairs to their apartment.

Her mother followed.

"Goodnight Mother." Razelle spoke softly.

Her mother gave her a curt nod, staring after her as she closed the door to her bedroom.

Distrust and a simmering impatience in her mother's words and actions had only gotten worse over the past few weeks.

Razelle didn't know how much longer she could live under this pressure.

If anything she felt more unloved and fearful with each passing day.

The only thing that saved her this past week was Luke's handwritten notes.

Every night for the past six days he'd written to her. He shared about what he was fixing in the cabin and about the housewarming they had for his mother. She had written that she was exhausted after working really long days at her Mother's cafe.

Raz even told him that someday she wanted to go see some of these places that she only read about in books.

They had got to know each other better through the messages they sent each other.

But Luke's note last night had been different.

After re-reading his note and even now as she waited, she was a pile of nerves. He'd written: *I have something important to ask you. See you tomorrow night at midnight. L.*

She lay in bed, pretending to be asleep when the door to her bedroom opened. She opened her eyes slightly, only to see her mother staring at her. When at last the door closed again, she sighed in relief.

Her mother had come to her bedroom to check on her almost every night since she'd begun her punishment.

Tears pricked her eyes.

She remembered a few times in her childhood when her Mother had been kind to her. But since she'd become an adult, things had changed. Now she was expected to work and to help her Mother heal from those disabling headaches.

Now that she was grown up, it seemed her Mother believed her only daughter no longer needed affection.

But that couldn't be further from the truth. She needed the love of a Mother now more than ever.

A light tap on her window made Razelle jerk suddenly out of bed.

Quickly wiping the tears from her eyes, she slowly opened the window.

Luke's smile quickly faded when he saw her. "Why have you been crying?"

"It's been a long day. I think I'm just tired."

He was silent for a long moment, his expression serious as he looked at her. "I think it's more than that. But, I'll let it go. I'm hoping that soon, you will feel like you can talk to me about anything."

What did he mean by that? Razelle had no idea, but she decided to let it go. He'd come here tonight for a specific reason.

"Your note said you wanted to ask me something?" She waited, rubbing her hands up and down on each arm to ward off the cool night air.

"Well first I need to tell you a cautionary tale." She nodded and Luke began. He told her of his great grandfather's death and about the stipulation in his will to marry by his twenty-seventh birthday if he wanted to inherit the land.

"When is your birthday?"

"I have two weeks left." Luke swallowed.

"You're right that is a cautionary tale." Razelle shook her head, the corners of her mouth turning up in a slight smile. "Well, two weeks isn't a lot of time."

"No it's not."

"Well then... what will you do?"

Luke stood up for a moment before kneeling down, a look of determination in the set of his jaw.

Razelle backed away from the window and one hand flew to her mouth. She silently shook her head. "No Luke. You aren't asking me what I think you are..."

He nodded. "Yes, I am. Marry me Razelle. This will be a fake marriage and something that will help us both. You'll have your freedom."

He reached for her hands, squeezing them gently. "Stay married to me for one year and I'll give you one million dollars. After the year is up, you'll have the freedom to do what you want." Luke's brown eyes searched hers with a sincerity that she found hard to resist.

Freedom. That word was like a foreign language to her. Something she'd never known. "I don't know what to say."

"Say yes, Raz." Luke persisted.

She studied him, surprise and shock lingering in her words. "A marriage of convenience. Do people do that sort of thing nowadays?"

"All I know is, it seems to be a thing in my family."

She shook her head from side to side thinking of the craziness of his idea and her for considering it.

All of a sudden she needed to hear from him again what his plans were. "And what exactly do you get out of this?"

"Grand's land. I've wanted that land since I was a little boy visiting the place with my Great-Grandfather, Granddad and my Dad. It's the one place I feel like I belong." Luke shrugged and looked away and Raz could sense a vulnerable place in him that she realized he probably didn't share with many people.

The longing in Luke's voice, resonated with the longing in her heart, but she couldn't tell him that. It's not like he was a complete stranger.

One of her best friends had married Luke's brother.

She knew this man came from a family that were committed to each other and treated people well. Not only that, he had already put his life on the line for her when they were at the camp.

Razelle believed she could trust him. But, it didn't take away the fact that she was consumed with fear and guilt at the thought of leaving her Mother.

But, doubt lingered at what he was asking of her.

"I just don't know if I can do that, Luke."

Luke leaned closer and whispered. "Just think about it Raz. That's all I'm asking. Will you do that?"

"All right. I can't promise to agree, but I can promise to think about it." Her voice caught in her throat at his whispered words.

"Thank you." Luke's gaze swept over her face one more time as if memorizing the way she looked right now. "I have to leave town for a couple days, but I'll be back in three days to take you away from here and marry you."

Raz stood there dumbfounded by his bold words. Before she could say anything however, he suddenly leaned over and kissed her cheek.

"I'll be back."

Warm tingles began in her cheek where he'd kissed her.

She put her hand on her cheek, her eyes glued to Luke as he disappeared into the dark night.

She was stunned at his idea of a marriage of convenience.

Was she crazy to even consider it?

CHAPTER SIX

uke

LUKE STARED into the dark night, looking up toward Raz's window.

There was no movement. There was no light. There was no sign at all that she was waiting for him.

It had been three days since he'd been here last. In that time, had she decided that marrying him wasn't a good idea after all?

He climbed the tree in silence, reaching the rooftop near her window.

Tapping lightly on her window, he straightened his shoulders, confident he was doing the right thing.

After a long wait, Razelle finally opened the window.

From the dim light inside her room, and he could see the shadowed outline of her form.

As she stepped closer, he saw her clearly.

Beautiful green eyes stared back at him, looking for all the world like she'd been crying.

"What's wrong?"

"Nothing." She hesitated and sighed. "Er — everything." His heartbeat accelerated and his palms grew sweaty at the catch in her voice.

She held up a handwritten note for him to see.

"That's good." It was a short note saying goodbye.

"No it's not good." Razelle took back the note with a shaky hand. "I'm afraid and really don't know if I should be doing this. I feel guilty for leaving."

"Why would you feel guilty?"

"Because she's my Mother." She quickly wiped away a stray tear that slipped down her cheek. "And because I remember all throughout my childhood that Mother told me: *I don't know what I'd do if you ever left me. I think I wouldn't want to live.*

Her brows puckered in worry. "I don't want to be responsible for my Mother choosing to end her life."

"You are not responsible for your Mother's emotions. Can't you see she's trying to manipulate you?" Luke saw this clearly because he'd been down this path before. His ex-fiance had tried to control him too.

Raz's eyes widened at his words.

Luke watched the play of emotions form across her face.

In a matter of seconds her expression went from fear, to shock and finally to anger.

All was quiet for a moment until suddenly heated whispered words escaped her lips. "You're right. My

Mother is trying to manipulate me. She's trying to control me to get me to stay with her forever. I won't let her use me like this."

She quickly turned and tossed her note on top of her dresser. Grabbing her backpack, she walked back to where he waited.

Her ragdoll cat jumped onto the bed.

Razelle reached for her cat, hugging her close.

"I'm ready."

Luke expelled a sigh of relief. "You're coming with me then."

It was a statement.

Green eyes stared back at him. Her eyes flashed and her jaw was set in determination before she nodded quickly.

Luke grinned and held out his hand to help her out of the window.

His heart accelerated as he held her small hand in his own.

A sudden, growing awareness blossomed inside of him that he had been entrusted with a very rare and precious gift.

One he needed to protect and nurture with all possible care.

HER BREATH WAS uneven as she shimmied down the tree.

Sunbeam squirmed in her arms. Luke stood on the ground, looking up as he waited.

Razelle couldn't believe she was actually doing this.

Her thoughts were erratic, coming and going with the rhythm of her heartbeat.

Was she doing the right thing?

All her life it had just been the two of them. She knew her Mother depended on her. It wasn't just that she helped at the coffee shop, but Razelle had learned how to help her Mother heal whenever she was having another one of her headaches.

Her mother relied on her.

What would she do now that her daughter was gone?

Guilt came back in full force.

What kind of terrible daughter was she to leave her Mother?

But along with the familiar stab of guilt, knots of fear formed in her belly.

Memories came back of times in her childhood when she had done something that displeased her Mother.

During those times, Mother had been unrelenting in the way she disciplined Razelle. Whether it was isolation, missed meals or lack of affection. All that punishment had formed craters of heartache on the inside.

She didn't want to experience that kind of pain again.

Maybe it was better she was leaving.

Suddenly, she was very grateful Luke was by her side.

At last her feet touched the ground. She swayed a little as one foot snagged on a tree branch. As she began to tilt sideways, suddenly strong arms wrapped around her back holding her steady.

Raz's head tipped back and she looked up to see Luke's brown eyes — warm like melted chocolate — so close to her own.

She sucked back air, momentarily surprised by his nearness.

"I've got you." His large hand on her back sent tingles along her spine and his warm breath tickled her cheek.

Her senses swelled to overflowing. Being so close to Luke she could smell the outdoorsy-garden smell she loved so much.

At Luke's words, the thought crossed her mind that she was in full agreement — she wouldn't mind staying here forever.

Hearing that thought vividly in her mind caused a jolt to run the length of her body. What was she thinking?

Raz struggled to steady her own two feet and heat filled her cheeks as her eyes met his. "Thanks."

"Anytime." Luke winked at her and grabbed her hand. "Let's get out of here."

Razelle anxiously looked over her shoulder at their home. She needed to look one last time.

There was no light in her Mother's upstairs bedroom. Good, she was safe for now.

Breathing a sigh of relief, Razelle hurried after Luke.

As he opened the truck door, she heard him ask. "Tomorrow we'll marry. But are you okay staying at my cabin until we take care of that?"

"Yes." She sat beside him and her grip tightened on her squirming cat. She whispered. "And, tomorrow I should call Cassie."

"Of course. I'll buy you a phone. We'll get things organized first thing in the morning." Luke's confident smile was the reassurance she needed.

He opened the truck door and led her into the small

two bedroom cabin. The dim lamp by the large wood front door, highlighted the comfy sofas that faced a large wood fireplace. The living room opened up to a spacious kitchen with rows of wood cabinets and warm yellow walls.

"This is a perfect spot. I love the fresh woodsy smell." Razelle smiled as she looked over at Luke.

"I'm happy you like it. The scent of wood is still fresh from the renovations I've been doing to the place." Luke shoved his hands in his pockets as he talked. Razelle caught the slightly red stain that coloured his cheeks as he shared what he'd been working on.

"Luke no one could have made this cabin better. It really is great." At her words a big grin formed on his face.

"Thanks." Luke looked over at her and she used one hand to cover a yawn. "But, here I am talking while you clearly are exhausted. Follow me." Luke led her into a bedroom that looked very cozy. The king sized bed dominated most of the room.

Pink blossomed in her cheeks. "But, this is your bedroom. I can sleep on the couch."

Ah yes, this was more like the Luke she was beginning to know. He was ever the gentleman.

"Yes. I'm giving you my bedroom and I'll sleep on the cot in the other bedroom. That other room is too cluttered with boxes and things. You'll be more comfortable here."

She nodded. "Okay."

"You're good?" Luke's brown eyes narrowed as he looked at her.

Tears pricked the back of her eyes.

Razelle felt a tear roll down her cheek and she hurriedly brushed it away with her sleeve. Her cat jumped out of her arms and soon curled up in a comfy spot on the bed. "I'm fine. It's just been a really long day."

Luke stepped closer until she was sure he could see the freckles on her nose.

His muscled arms wrapped around her and he held her gently in his arms. Razelle couldn't remember the last time anyone gave her a hug just to help her feel better.

Tears ran down her cheeks.

His heartfelt gesture seared its way into her heart, and her heart opened a little further to him.

Who was this man? He had the ability to chase down thugs, to help his friends and only a few days later here he was holding her in his arms.

His gentle hug wrapped its way around her heart, chipping away at fears she'd kept bottled up for so long. She could feel her heart opening up in a new way to his kindness.

As Razelle rested her head against his shoulder, she didn't want to move away. For the first time in a long time, she felt safe and cared for.

She forced herself to step back. She couldn't let herself be attracted to him.

He handed her a tissue. "Thank you Luke. I don't know where all those water works came from. I probably just need a good sleep." Razelle peered up at him through wet lashes, and stepping back a little further.

"I'm sure that's true. I won't keep you any longer. Goodnight Raz. I'll see you in the morning." Luke walked out of the bedroom and with one last lingering smile closed the door.

She stood there frozen. Warmth flooded her neck and rose to her face. Her body still felt the weight of his hands as though they were still wrapped around her.

And Heaven help her, she wanted to feel his arms around her again.

Suddenly she realized that her initial attraction to Luke had now blossomed into so much more.

She needed to rein in her feelings. She couldn't allow herself to fall for the man she was about to marry.

A mixture of emotions warred on the inside. Fear and uncertainty mixed with relief knowing that she was no longer under her Mother's thumb.

Now, she no longer had to worry about her Mother, at least she hoped that was true.

At least right now, her Mother didn't know where she was. But, she knew it was only a matter of time before she found out.

At this moment, Razelle was very uncertain. Uncertain about her future. Uncertain about her Mother. And uncertain about this new marriage-in-name-only to Luke Stevenson.

Tomorrow would be the beginning of many firsts in her life.

Razelle didn't know if she was ready for all the changes that lay ahead of her.

Would she ever truly find the love and belonging she was looking for?

❧

LUKE SHIFTED HIS FEET, his gaze moving from the pastor and back to his family.

It had been a busy day, getting the details organized for the small private wedding ceremony.

He smiled at his Grandmom and Mother who sat together.

Luke was grateful for a supportive family, even when details of his life — like getting married — happened quickly.

If it had been up to him, they would have been married at the office of the Justice of the Peace.

But, that wouldn't have been a good idea, especially if he wanted to convince his mom and grandparents they were in love.

He was grateful Catherine Stevenson had used her connections to ask the pastor here on such short notice.

Not to mention, GrandMom insisted Razelle wear her old wedding dress.

His mother winked at him and he shifted his feet once again. He suddenly remembered being in this position years ago, when the woman he loved left him at the altar.

This time around, he was marrying without love. Yet, even though this was a marriage that would benefit them both, Razelle could still decide not to go through with it.

Anxiety formed knots in his belly.

Had his wife-to-be decided to run away?

He rubbed clammy hands on his suit pants and swallowed nervously.

They were already five minutes late and Luke was worried. The waiting seemed to go on forever.

Without warning, the music started playing in the background.

He looked at the row of poplar trees that surrounded Grand's old cabin, waiting.

Suddenly, his bride stepped through to the other side, her hand tucked behind Granddad's arm.

Luke expelled a breath of relief and his eyes widened at the sight of her.

Razelle was stunning.

The wait had definitely been worth it.

She wore a floor length dress with wide skirts that tapered upwards to her slim waist. The scooped neckline and lace-covered long sleeves only accented her slender frame.

His bride's thick wavy auburn hair hung past her waist, flowing gently with every graceful step she took toward him.

The vintage lace wedding veil sloped over her shoulders and down her back. The long train of her wedding dress shimmered like a heavenly canopy of diamonds.

It seemed appropriate that the beauty of nature surrounded them on this, their wedding day.

Luke remained motionless as his bride glided the rest of the way toward him. He nodded his thanks and swallowed back emotion as his Granddad placed Razelle's hand in his.

He squeezed her hand.

A flicker of fear momentarily shone in her big green eyes and he gave her a reassuring smile as they turned to face the pastor.

It didn't seem to take the minister very long before he got to the part where they said their vows.

"Do you Luke Stevenson take Razelle Chattaine to be your lawfully wedded wife, to have and to hold from this day forward...?" Luke listened to the rest of the wedding vows as the pastor recited them.

His conscience prodded him as he replied. "I... I I do." Emotion welled up on the inside, causing him to stutter.

The vow to protect, honor and take care of his new wife was easily given.

Love, on the other hand, was a feeling he needed to stay far away from.

Problem was, his attraction to his bride couldn't be denied.

Last night, he had wanted to hold her in his arms longer. She had pulled away much too quickly, and Luke sensed his bride wasn't used to the people in her life showing her much affection.

As Razelle whispered her vows to him, Luke found himself eager to hold her in his arms once again.

Finally the Pastor spoke the words he'd been waiting for. "You may kiss the bride."

With slightly shaky hands, he lifted the lacy veil that covered her face.

Razelle's wide green eyes looked into his own, flickering with doubt and worry.

He wanted to settle her worries and bring comfort to his new wife.

Luke stepped closer and placed one hand on her waist while the other cradled the back of her head.

He stared into her eyes a moment longer. There was no question his bride was beautiful.

Without waiting, his mouth came down on hers with an intensity that surprised even him. Burrowing his hand into her hair, he weaved his fingers through the silken tresses, as if binding her to him.

At her low moan, he gentled his kisses for fear of hurting her. But, the soft womanly feel of her was overpowering. In the end, he kissed her over and over again until his heart rate accelerated and seemed like it was about to burst straight out of his chest.

Luke lost himself in his bride's sweetness and at that moment could feel the years of loneliness melt away.

It was a sensation that was brand new and he could feel his body quivering filled with new emotions. He liked being close to his new wife a little too much.

What was happening to him?

Whatever it was, he needed to put a stop to the new surge of attraction for Razelle. This wasn't part of the deal they'd agreed on.

He stepped back and stared down at the beautiful woman in front of him.

Heaven help him, all he wanted to do was kiss her all over again.

WITH EACH ONE of Luke's kisses, the ragged pounding of Razelle's heart rose higher and higher, until the roar filled her ears.

Nothing in her life had given her a sensation as potent as her new husband's kisses.

As his lips explored her own, she closed her eyes revelling in the new sensations he created inside her.

Her hands shook against his shoulders and slid up around his neck.

She pulled his head closer, wanting more of his sweet kisses.

Luke's hands tangled in her hair gently and she went weak kneed from his caresses.

A low moan escaped her lips.

The finest of wines couldn't produce a sensation like this.

Razelle trembled in his arms and he pulled his lips from hers.

His gaze met hers. Large brown eyes stared at her filled with turbulence and confusion.

The look in his eyes only reflected the chaos inside her.

As the pastor pronounced them husband and wife, Luke turned to the small group of wedding guests.

Razelle followed his example, pasting a smile to her lips.

All too soon, Luke's brothers and their wives embraced her. She felt accepted into their close circle, something that surprised her.

Luke's mother reached out and pulled her into a close embrace and kissed her cheek. "Welcome to the family, Razelle. I'm thrilled you've married my son and I really look forward to getting to know you better."

"Thank you Mrs. Stevenson." Tears pricked the back of Raz's eyes. There was only one other person in her life that had treated her so special — her childhood Grandmere who took care of her when they lived on Moorea Island.

Her husband's mother treated her with an unexpected kindness that caused her heart to overflow.

"I'd love it if you'd call me Mom, my dear. We're family now, after all." Eliza Stevenson winked and squeezed her hand.

"I'd like that. Thank you Mom." Razelle's lips trembled a little by the unconditional acceptance she experienced from Luke's family. It wasn't long before Catherine and William Stevenson both embraced her.

Today, she'd been taken into their close-knit family.

Soon, her friend Cassie grabbed her into a hug, a lopsided grin on her face. "This was the fastest wedding ever. You're sure you don't have something you need to tell me?"

"Cassie, you know I already explained." Razelle sighed heavily.

"I know, I know. You are helping each other out." Cassie leaned closer to whisper in her ear. "But, the way Luke's eyes follow you, it certainly doesn't look like a marriage-of-convenience to me."

Her friend grinned and planted a quick kiss on her cheek.

"You're crazy. He's not looking at me in any way, other than as a friend." Razelle didn't need her best friend to assume things that weren't real. Besides if Luke were attracted to her, Raz would've noticed. Wouldn't she?

Cassie blew her a kiss and walked over to chat with Rory.

Razelle sighed, feeling a little frustrated by their conversation.

"You okay?" Luke looked over at her and placed his hand around her waist, tugging her to his side.

At his touch, a jolt of awareness went through her.

Her new husband led her to the wooden dance floor.

It was tradition for the bride and groom to have the first dance. Raz's fingers nervously toyed with her wedding dress.

The atmosphere around them was more romantic than she anticipated and it was wreaking havoc with her peace of mind.

Music played softly in the background. Luke must have arranged the last minute for people to bring what they needed.

Lights shimmered and twinkled in different places around the back yard.

"It's our turn." Luke placed his large hand on the small of her back as they settled in the middle of the dance floor. A country singer crooned a love song and he pulled her close.

"You are beautiful tonight." Luke whispered before he gently pulled her close.

Heat rose from her neck and blossomed in her cheeks.

She'd never had so many compliments in her life, than what she'd received since knowing Luke. She realized, her new husband might be a man of few words, but the ones he took advantage of were definitely put to good use.

"Thank you Luke. You look good yourself." Razelle had never seen him look more handsome than he did tonight.

His perfectly tailored suit and along with his expensive looking watch, cufflinks and leather shoes, looked so good on him that it had sparked both attraction and fear in her chest.

The mixture of emotions she experienced whenever he was near, scared her.

Luke was a billionaire and adept at the way things worked among the world of the wealthy. But, sadly the woman he married didn't know the first thing about how to dress, how to act or how to be part of his life.

She was certain it wouldn't be long before her husband realized it too. When he did, he would understand that she didn't belong in his world.

Suddenly, Luke pulled her closer and kissed the top of her head, his muscular arms wrapped around her waist.

Razelle started to pull away from him, but he tightened his arms around her waist, rubbing one hand on the small of her back.

"Stay. Please?" He pulled back slightly so he could look into her eyes. "We're newlyweds and supposed to be in love, remember?" The circular motion of his hand on her back and his whispered words had their desired effect.

Being in her husband's arms brought up a yearning for more than a marriage-in-name-only.

"Sorry. You're right." She spoke softly. Silently she chastised herself for letting her emotions get away from her.

It was part of the deal they'd made for this marriage.

Without warning, he gently placed her arms around

his neck, pulling her closer. "I think we need to be more convincing."

Luke's brown eyes crinkled at the edges and the corners of his lips turned up. She couldn't help but offer a small smile in return, even though being so close to him made her feel so vulnerable.

Leaning his head down, her new husband placed a gentle kiss on her forehead, her eyelids and at last his mouth landed on her own. Hungrily his lips nipped and pulled, devouring hers until her whole body felt like liquid jelly.

As her knees started to weaken from his lingering kiss, Razelle forced herself to pull her arms away from around his neck.

"I think we've convinced them." She whispered and stepped back a little to put some distance between them.

She was very afraid that their kisses had begun to convince her heart that maybe it would be possible for them to fall in love.

But no, that couldn't ever happen.

More than ever, Razelle knew she needed to put walls up around her heart.

She needed to do whatever it took, to avoid being hurt by someone she loved ever again.

As Razelle stepped away from him, Luke couldn't help but be overcome by a sense of loss.

He didn't understand why he would feel this way, especially since he was just getting to know his new wife.

Luke's heart leapfrogged into his throat and he wanted to grab her back into his arms. But something told him to leave well enough alone.

The fact that Raz stepped away from him was probably for the best.

Maybe this way, he could ignore his attraction to his wife.

Maybe this way, he could ignore his longing to know his wife.

Maybe this way, he could ignore his desire to love his wife.

CHAPTER SEVEN

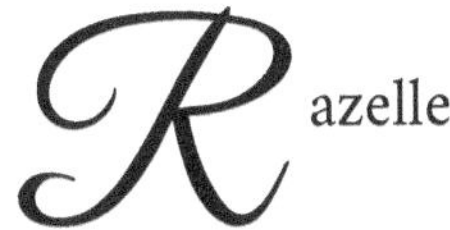azelle

R**AZELLE INHALED DEEPLY** of the familiar scent of the ocean as their Porter led the way into their hotel room that overlooked the ocean.

Since leaving early this morning, the plane had finally landed an hour ago in Papeete, Tahiti in the French Polynesian Islands.

"Enjoy your stay. Let me know how else I can serve you." Luke handed the man a large tip and he bowed before quietly leaving.

Razelle shifted her gaze to Luke, peering at him through thick eyelashes. Rubbing her hand on her jean shorts, she did her best to erase evidence of nervousness.

Her belly had been in knots ever since last night's wedding ceremony. Luke was busy responding to a message on his Smartphone, so Razelle took that moment to walk out to the balcony.

The view of the vivid blue ocean surrounding them was incredible.

She sighed, enjoying the salty breeze that loosened strands of hair from her thick braid.

Light footsteps sounded behind her.

She turned slightly and shifted her arms from their resting place against the railing.

"So what do you think?" Luke's gaze encompassed the ocean, the beach and the tropical paradise that surrounded them.

"It's beautiful." Razelle was surprised when he'd finally told her on the plane where they were going. Mixed feelings bubbled up as memories came back of her childhood in Tahiti.

"Not half as beautiful as you." Heat rushed up to her cheeks at his compliment.

"Thank you Luke." That's all she could think of to say. Throughout her life, she'd rarely received any type of appreciation.

In all honesty, she wasn't sure what to say or even if she should take his words seriously. Growing up she'd learned the hard way from Mother, that she wasn't good enough to receive such compliments.

He must have realized his words made her uncomfortable, because suddenly he switched topics.

"Happy to be back?" A glimmer of sparkle shone in his brown eyes.

Razelle brows puckered together as she struggled to

still her troubled memories. She smiled and nodded briefly. "How did you know?"

"Cassie mentioned it. I thought you might like to come back for a visit."

She didn't say anything and instead glanced at her new husband with a barely-there smile on her face.

There were so many things Luke didn't know about her. Maybe this vacation would help them learn more about each other. She hoped so. But tonight wasn't the night for deep discussions.

She put a hand over her mouth to cover a yawn.

"I'm sorry, you must be tired. I forgot about the time difference from Seattle to Tahiti." Luke opened the sliding door to take them back inside their hotel.

"It's okay." Razelle walked into the main area of their hotel suite. "But, I think I'll turn in so I've got more energy for tomorrow."

Luke grinned. "You're going to need it. I've got a few treats planned for us."

Razelle raised one eyebrow surprised he'd had any time to plan at all with how quickly they got married.

"That'll be fun. I look forward to it." She quickly nodded and opened the door to her bedroom.

Leaning her head against the back of the door, she sighed.

Her thoughts raced a mile a minute and her emotions were all in a tangle. Being close to Luke — with his surprising compliments and kindnesses — was beginning to soften the edges around her heart.

Razelle realized she would have to keep a close guard

on her heart, so she wouldn't do what she feared the most… fall for her husband.

§.

A SLIGHT BREEZE blew loose tendrils of hair against Razelle's cheeks as the Catamaran boat skipped across the water, nearing their destination.

Luke shifted his body, moving closer until his thigh touched hers. "I thought we could spend most of the week at Moorea Island. It's not that far from Papeete. I was told it has amazing views."

"It is beautiful." She lifted one hand to shade her eyes from the bright morning sun and sighed at the majesty of the mountains of Moorea Island in the distance. This Island was one she knew well. This place held some of her fondest memories from childhood. And now she was back. So many memories flooded her thoughts, causing mixed emotions.

"I agree." Luke's deep voice whispered in her ear.

She turned toward him and heat crawled from her neck to her cheeks as her husband's brown eyes darkened and focused intensely on her. She could hardly believe this man thought she was beautiful.

Blinking away the pricking of tears behind her eyes, she forced herself to smile as she focused on the striking landscape in front of her.

After so many years of being criticized and told she wasn't much to look at, she had come to accept it as true.

Once again, she told herself he was just being kind. But his words were thoughtful all the same.

Swallowing back the clog of emotions that lodged in her throat Razelle sent him a quick sideways glance and whispered. "Thank you."

Turning her head, she watched as the captain guided their boat to the dock while her hands fidgeted with her jean shorts.

Luke must have sensed her discomfort, because he quickly changed the subject. Pointing to an inlet of water surrounded by beautiful green foliage, he said. "See that spot over there? That's where we'll be going later today."

Razelle's gaze followed the place he indicated. Clear blue-green water surrounded the area and many different shapes and sizes of fish circled the coral below.

"I've been checking out fun things to do, and I thought we could go hiking, explore the outer part of the Island from a sea-doo and of course snorkelling. There's supposed to be incredible coral reefs and tropical fish to see."

"I look forward to it." Even though she lived here as a small girl, they never had the money to go do any of the interesting things offered to tourists.

As they stepped off the boat and walked toward the beach, Luke kept his hand on the small of her back.

Tingles of warmth spread up her back at his touch. She made a mental note: *Don't get used to this. It's not like Luke cares for you. He's just being kind and protective.*

Soon they stopped and Luke talked to someone at the hotel and soon a concierge handed them the swipe card that was the key to their room. They walked along the wooden walkway, to the one of the overwater bungalows situated in deeper waters.

"No way." Raz's eyes widened and she turned to Luke when she saw where they were headed. "We're staying in one of the overwater cabins?"

Luke grinned, his brown eyes sparkling. "Yeah. I thought this would be the best way to make the most of our time here. You like?"

Razelle quickly nodded. "I do."

Green foliage surrounded the walkway leading up to the A frame wooden lodge.

As they stepped inside, she was amazed by all the details the hotel took care of for them.

Running her fingers along one of two soft cotton white bathrobes in the spacious closet, she sighed.

Next to it was a coffee maker with more than enough coffee for each day of their stay. Opening the mini-bar beneath it, she was happy to see bottled water as well as their favorite sodas and beverages included.

Straight across from the mini-fridge, was the bathroom.

She especially loved the claw-foot bathtub and the double sinks.

The bungalow was built with beautiful natural wood, giving it an authentic tropical island feel.

She followed Luke to the other room, only to see him wave for her to come over.

"Look down. You can see the water beneath our bungalow."

Stepping near the glass panel on the floor, she looked down and gasped in surprise. "There's a glass panel on the floor. That's incredible." It felt surreal and made her a little dizzy to see the fish and coral under the floor of their room.

"Yeah." His shoulder bumped hers playfully as he leaned closer looking into the clear blue water below.

Suddenly, he grabbed her hand. "The view from the deck is just as incredible."

Luke pulled her to his side as they walked onto the deck, slipping his hand lightly around her waist.

Surprised, she laughed and followed him outside.

Warm tingles spread outward from where his hand rested against her. She needed to focus her attention off of Luke.

She leaned against the wooden rail, peering out at the ocean in front of her. Blue sky met the blue of the ocean until you couldn't tell where one ended and the other began.

Watching the mountains of Moorea Island to the side and the tropical fish below was mesmerizing.

Even though Razelle remembered coming to the beach as a child, being here now as an adult experiencing it with her husband, added a whole new depth of meaning.

Luke suddenly turned his head a happy and relaxed grin in place.

"It's good?"

"It's good. This view is incredible."

Luke started to take off his shirt and threw it on the deck. He looked over at her grinning playfully. "I don't think I can wait."

Razelle picked up her smartphone, turned on the video and followed Luke. He ran down the wood steps that led to the main level deck and jumped into the aquamarine water.

The water only came up to his chest.

As he started to swim, he called out. "Razelle, come join me."

She took a few more photos of him before setting her smartphone down on top of a nearby table.

"I'm coming."

It was a good thing she had put her swimsuit on under her clothes before they left this morning. Hurriedly she slipped out of her t-shirt and jean shorts and jumped in the water.

Surfacing, she bumped into Luke's muscled chest. She placed her hands on his chest to keep her balance. Heat rose up, staining her cheeks.

Luke took her hand and raised his eyes to hers, kissing the inside of her hand. The sensation of his lips on her palm made Razelle gasp.

"I shouldn't be doing this." He groaned, and with a gentle hand directed her face toward his. He kissed her forehead, her eyelids and her cheeks.

For a moment, they broke apart. But, Luke leaned close to her again and Razelle met him halfway. This time when their lips came together it went much deeper.

All of a sudden she was lost in wave after wave of sensation as his lips melded with her own. When he lifted his head, for a moment she was disoriented and sensed that he was a little shocked, just as she was.

Their kiss was much better than either of them could have expected.

Luke pulled back, his hands gripping her shoulders.

His eyes had darkened to a chocolate brown, turbulent and intense as his gaze met hers.

"I'm sorry." His words erupted out of his lips, his breaths shallow and uneven.

Razelle was light headed and still reeling from the intensity of his kiss, that she barely caught his hushed words.

It seemed to her, by the force of emotions that played across his face, that he regretted their kiss.

"It's okay Luke." Still reeling from his passionate kiss, she desperately needed to do something to escape the conflicting emotions that rose up inside her. "Why don't we go snorkelling like you planned?"

A look of relief settled on Luke's face.

"We should. I thought we could go to the Lagoon. It's where many tourists go to look at the sea creatures. I'll get our snorkelling gear." Luke swam to the deck and reached to pull her up to the deck with him.

They hurried to put on shorts and t-shirts and then grabbing their underwater masks and snorkelling gear, they took the water ferry to the small island a short distance from Moorea Island.

Sitting beside Luke in the boat, she was quiet and couldn't help but feel the sting of rejection from Luke's earlier words. His passionate kisses had made her toes curl, then why did he act remorseful now?

She forced herself to shake off feelings of confusion, rejection and anger.

Arriving at the Lagoon they followed the guide who led them to their destination.

Throwing her shoulders back, she determined to take

her focus off her fake husband and onto the fact that they were here to have a fun vacation.

Reaching for her snorkelling mask and flippers she put them on.

The underwater mask kept slipping as she tried to adjust it on her face.

"I had trouble fixing mine too. Let me help." Luke spoke softly and gently adjusted her strap until it fit properly.

"Thanks Luke." Why did he have to be so nice? Now, she felt like a bad person for being upset with him in the first place.

They got into the water and along with two other tourists and began to swim where the fish were.

Before long Luke was swimming beside her. He pointed to the baby sharks and stingrays that were swimming in a circle not far from where they were.

Their guide had assured them that it was safe to swim with and feed the sharks, stingrays and the other types of fish.

Razelle was happy they were told to grab the strong cable lines in the water if they felt the water current became too strong.

She gripped the line tightly, watching the multi-colored fish swim all around her.

Luke swam close to her, his eyes sparkling with laughter. It seemed he was having the time of his life.

She had to admit, being up close to these sea creatures, even though a little intimidating, it was still beautiful.

When they swam back to shore, Raz grinned at Luke. "That was like an underwater sea life extravaganza."

"Sure was. Happy we came?" Luke asked as he handed her a towel to dry off.

"I am. Thanks Luke, that was a lot of fun." Without warning her stomach gurgled loudly. She giggled and placed a hand over her belly.

"Hungry?" She nodded and grinned as Luke grabbed her hand as they walked to the ferryboat that waited to take them back. "How about if we have a picnic on the beach?"

"I'd like that."

Soon, the boat took them to the outdoor grill restaurant on Cocoa Beach.

Razelle remembered coming here a few times with her Grandmere.

"Bonjour, Mademoiselle." The dark haired man spoke to them from under the fringe of the outdoor cabana.

"Bonjour." Razelle responded automatically in French.

Luke raised an eyebrow as he looked at her.

"If you're curious, I said it's a beautiful day and asked what their food of the day was." Heat stained her cheeks. It felt weird to speak in another language in front of Luke.

After asking Luke what foods he liked, she placed their order.

The man replied quickly.

Razelle smiled and replied. "Merci beaucoup."

She turned to Luke. "He said one of their servers will arrive at our table with our food and drinks."

"That's great. Thanks for ordering for both of us." They walked to a picnic table located on the sandy beach and sat down.

Before long a woman with long dark hair with beautiful olive skin brought their food and drinks.

"Merci." Razelle smiled at the woman who bowed her head slightly before she walked away.

"I'm amazed. I'm probably one of the few American tourists who gets to visit these French Islands with a beautiful wife who speaks fluent French." Luke grinned at her.

Razelle was pleased with his compliment. A thrill shot up her spine and heat stained her cheeks. "Well, it's been a long time since I spoke the language, but it seems to be coming back."

She took a bite of her parrotfish that had been grilled in the outdoor grill. "This food is so good. How's your grilled lobster?"

"It's good. This lobster alongside the passion fruit margarita drink, is the best meal I've had in a long time." Luke grinned at her, a relaxed almost boyish expression softening his face.

"Is this the first time in awhile that you've truly relaxed?"

Luke took a sip of his drink and looked out at the clear blue water, before he looked back at her, a deep soulful expression in his dark brown eyes. "Yeah. It's been a little busy fixing up Grand's cabin last year. I promised the people who have been interested in my financial software and courses, that I would stick to a monthly budget of the average American for one full year."

"That's inspiring. So, that's why you did the work yourself?" Razelle knew he was worth a few billion, so she found it incredible that he would volunteer to put himself on a strict budget.

"Yes. It wasn't easy but it was worth it. I just finished up the full year at the end of last week." Luke tossed her a sheepish grin. "I was surprised there were people who shared they'd been following my minimalist lifestyle and had been inspired to do the same. It helped them get out of debt."

"That's really great Luke. That's something I'm happy I learned about you." Razelle studied him thoughtfully.

They stood to their feet and began walking.

"Now, it's your turn. I want to hear more about you. For instance, what was life like as a child in these islands?" Luke threw her a sideways grin that seemed a little more like a challenge than a passing question.

Razelle cocked a half-grin his way. "All right. I guess that's a fair question since you told me a little of your story."

Luke chuckled softly and bumped his shoulder playfully against hers. "Yes, it is."

She threw him a half-smile and swished her feet through the water as they walked.

Memories came back from when she first came to the island and she puckered her brows together.

"I vaguely remember when we first arrived on the big island. We lived in Papeete for a time and all I remember was Mother being gone a lot and that I had many different babysitters everyday during that first year or so. It wasn't until I was almost four that we moved to Moorea Island. That's when Mother met Grandmere." Razelle smiled, releasing a soft sigh.

"Sounds like happy memories."

"Yes. The best years I remember were with Grandmere." She looked at the white sandy beach ahead.

"In fact the beach was our favourite place to go. We'd often come across people she knew, but sometimes it would just be Grandmere and me just having fun together." She bent down to retrieve a rock from the sandy beach, staring down at it in the palm of her hand.

"She would point out unique rocks and would encourage me to bring my favorites back to her house. I had quite a collection."

Suddenly a white and orange striped fish clownfish popped his head above the water. Razelle giggled at the sight.

"It is kind of cute. Looks a little like orange and white striped fish from that kids movie." Luke stopped beside her to watch them play in the water.

Razelle nodded, sighing happily. "I remember Grandmere would tell me about the different fish and other sea creatures. Ever so often we would come across the endangered green sea turtles as they trudged slowly into the water to eat their sea grass and algae. I loved spending time with her. She taught me so many things."

"You must have missed your mother. Did she work long hours?"

At Luke's question, a stab of pain seared her heart. "Yeah. Most days she wouldn't pick me up from Grandmere's until almost midnight and then we'd go to our tiny one room apartment. It was dark there. I remember being scared a lot and was always so happy when I got to stay overnight at Grandmere's house."

They continued walking and Luke placed a hand on the small of her back.

A familiar brooding look formed on his face and his brows pinched together in concern.

"Do you think your Grandmere is still on the Island?"

"I don't know. I wrote to her after we moved back to the States, but she never wrote me back. I thought maybe she was mad at me, or didn't want anything to do with me anymore." It hurt still to think about it.

She had grown to love Grandmere and wished she would have written me back.

"Should we see if she still lives here?"

Razelle hesitated and finally nodded. "I'm unsure if she'll want to see me, but I would like to see her again."

"From what you've told me about her, I'm convinced your Grandmere will be happy to see you again." Luke put his arm gently around her shoulders and pulled her to him.

He kissed the top of her head, pulling her closer. "Don't worry, we'll find her."

Silent tears streamed down her face as she was wrapped in Luke's arms.

His gentle embrace and concern for her feelings caused her to come undone. It had been a long time since anyone had really taken the time to listen and to really care.

Even her worry of seeing Grandmere again diminished because she was confident Luke would be by her side.

At that moment, Razelle couldn't deny her fake husband had cracked a little more of the ice that had encased her heart for years.

What would she do if he melted it altogether?

CHAPTER EIGHT

uke

Luke knocked on the old clapboard door again.

Beside him Raz's fingers shook slightly as she fingered the flower shaped key that hung on the gold chain around her neck.

Her dusty green eyes shifted up to him and he found his face lifting in warmth at her gaze.

"It'll be okay." He squeezed the cold hand, which gripped his like a lifeline.

He knocked once more, thinking that perhaps she wasn't home, when suddenly the door opened. The rusty hinges squeaked.

Standing on with the screen door open, stood a much older white haired lady with beautiful olive skin.

She wore a simple traditional Polynesian dress that

hung to her ankles. The bright red colors with yellow flowers and green leaves gave Luke the impression that this woman was very much a part of the island around her.

She first looked at Luke and nodded quickly before turning her gaze to Razelle.

An unexpected gasp escaped from the older woman's lips and her wrinkled hand quickly covered her mouth.

"Ma enfant cherie." The old lady's brown eyes shone brightly and the corners of her mouth turned up forming deep grooves in her skin. She reached over and grabbed Razelle into a tight embrace.

Even though he didn't understand the language, he could tell by the reaction of both women that they were more than happy to see each other.

The atmosphere lightened, and a glow of warmth seeped into him. Luke felt keenly aware that this was a moment to remember.

Finally Razelle — who he could tell had some painful memories — was seeing some happiness in her life.

He was thrilled to be the one to bring a smile to her beautiful face.

As Razelle stepped out of the tight embrace of her Grandmere, sparks of happiness shot up her nerve endings, making her feel like a giddy child again.

"Come in, come in." Grandmere spoke quickly and waved them inside the house. Razelle did her best to translate for Luke as they spoke. "Come sit outside on the deck. Who is the man beside you?"

"He's my husband, Mamie." Razelle reverted quickly back to the familiar name she called her Grandmere as a little child.

"His name is Luke." She felt a little strange calling Luke her husband, knowing that Mamie would think he was her husband in every sense of the word. She didn't like to deceive the one woman who had given her so much, but right now it couldn't be helped.

"Your husband? Oh, how wonderful ma cherie." Grandmere's brown eyes twinkled and her lips turned up into a large smile.

Heat rose up to her cheeks. "Thank you Mamie."

"Come, let's sit in the comfortable chairs and you can tell me how you and your Mother are doing." Mamie gave them each a glass of her sweetened iced tea.

Razelle took a long sip and sighed. "This is so good Mamie. Just like I remember."

"So tell me Razelle, how are you?"

"I'm good. I've been working in Mother's Cafe for years now. She's made a success of it, just like she wanted."

"Good, good." But Mamie's eyes gave her a calculated look. "But you my dear? How have you been?"

Razelle paused. "I've gotten very tired of working for Mother quite honestly. I don't mean to sound ungrateful, Mamie. I'm thankful for all that Mother has helped me with through the years, but I think what's happened is I've grown up. Now I long for more freedom." Razelle began to explain to Grandmere about the long hours and that she wasn't able to get out much to visit with friends.

Her gaze met Mamie's who nodded and sent her a sad little smile. "I understand completely. It is time for you to have more of your freedom and more friends."

Something about Mamie's voice made her pause and she waited. Grandmere continued cautiously.

"Something you didn't know when you lived here years ago as a child, is that your Mother was very protective of you. She explained to me when I first agreed to care for you, that you were her only daughter and she didn't want anyone — especially anyone English — to be involved in your life." Grandmere paused shaking her head.

She went on. "She asked back then if I would keep you away from any adults. She agreed to let you play with children your age, but she was very strict about not letting any other adults into your life."

Razelle nodded. "Hmm. She's always been incredibly protective of me."

"I see in your eyes, that it's been hard on you ma cherie." A faraway look was in the older woman's eyes. "Did your Mother let you have more friends as you grew up? Where did you live?"

Razelle sighed heavily, unsure of what to tell her. It had been so many years since they'd talked. "Don't you remember Mamie? I explained in my letters to you where we lived and what we were doing."

"What letters? I didn't receive any letters from you my dear." Grandmere's brows pressed together in confusion.

"You didn't get them?" Razelle remembered writing almost every week for months after they moved to the States, but when Grandmere didn't write back, she thought maybe her precious Mamie was glad to finally be rid of her.

Luke listened as she translated and the conversation for him. He sighed. "Are you sure your Mother mailed the letters you wrote?"

Razelle translated Luke's words for Grandmere and her eyes widened. "Razelle, do you think your Mother didn't want you to write to me for some reason?"

As difficult as that question was to hear, Razelle had to admit her Mother had been so worried throughout her childhood of anyone getting too close to her daughter. But, why would Mother not want her to write to Grandmere? That didn't make any sense.

"I can't think of any reason why Mother wouldn't want me to write to you Mamie." Razelle shook her head. A sudden anger reared its ugly head inside of her as her Mother's face flitted across her eyes.

How could her own Mother lie to her? Had she thrown out all those letters Razelle had spent days writing to Grandmere?

"Hmm. Ma cherie, maybe your mother was scared?"

Razelle shook her head. "I don't think so. Mother hasn't been scared a day in her life."

"Ah, well then you don't know her as well as you think."

"What do you mean, Mamie?"

Grandmere got that faraway look in her eyes. "I remember when your Mother first brought you to me to ask me to care for you Razelle. You were so small and afraid of almost everything and everyone. But, when I looked into your Mother's eyes, I saw fear."

"Mother was scared? Of what?"

"During my time of taking care of you, your Mother would tell me little pieces of her past that helped me understand." Grandmere sighed heavily before she continued.

"Your mother told me she'd done some things that weren't quite legal back where she'd come from and so she had come to Moorea Island looking to start over." She paused as she remembered.

"I don't know what she meant, but it would explain why your Mother seemed like she was always looking over her shoulder."

Razelle sucked in a deep breath. "What do you think Mother would've meant by that?"

"Maybe all is not as it seems from the outside looking in. Perhaps there were other reasons why your Mother kept you hidden away and protected?" Luke interjected, voicing the same questions that swirled in her head.

A furrow formed between Razelle's brows as troubled thoughts caused more questions than she had answers for.

"Now ma cherie, let's talk about something to help take away the worry lines on your forehead." Grandmere reached over and with a gentle hand touched her puckered brows.

The corners around her brown eyes crinkled as a gentle smile filled her face.

Too many emotions welled up trying to clog her throat. She swallowed back tears and nodded, determined that she wouldn't think about all her Mother had done. Instead, she would enjoy this time with her Grandmere.

"Well, since we're changing the subject, I'd love to hear

more about my wife's childhood." Luke spoke, grinning mischievously at her.

Raz tossed her husband a salty look, letting him know he was treading on dangerous territory, but translated his words anyway to Grandmere.

"Oh, do I have stories." Grandmere grinned.

Razelle sighed with a grimace. She was not looking forward to being embarrassed in front of Luke.

Grandmere pointed a crooked finger to the dirt road that led to the neighbor's homes. "I remember one summer when Razelle was six years old, we were at the park with the other villagers."

Mamie smiled as she remembered. "In the middle of our party, she noticed some people carrying fireworks. She watched as they set one off as a test. And when those villagers responsible for the fireworks weren't looking, Razelle snuck behind them and ignited one of them."

"There was such a fuss afterwards. A few villagers were angry. And I needed to explain to my little one that it wasn't safe to play with fireworks."

Memories of the beautiful lights in the sky that night came back to Razelle.

"Afterwards, all my little girl said was that she made pretty lights in the sky." Grandmere laughed out loud and the familiar belly laugh brought back memories of all the fun times she'd had as a child laughing and playing with Mamie.

"Well it was pretty."

Luke chuckled. "So the pluck you have now, started when you were just a child. You haven't changed much."

Razelle giggled realizing it was true.

When she translated Luke's words, Grandmere asked why he would say she hadn't changed much.

"Well, you might not know it, but a few years ago when Raz was told there was a camp where the homeless lived outside of our town, she started to go there to visit." Luke looked her way and winked.

"Then she started going at nights after she finished at the coffee shop to bring food and bring her herbs and other natural remedies to help those who were sick to heal."

"Ah, that's my Razelle. Compassion for the less fortunate has always been her nature." Grandmere smiled and patted her hand.

Mamie began to share more memories. "I remember one time when her neighbor friend Maria got sick and was in bed for weeks, Razelle asked all of her other friends to donate a toy or stuffed animal. In two days they had a bagful, which they took to Maria. Your friend was so happy and it wasn't long before she was better. You remember?"

"Yes Mamie, I remember."

"I'm glad." Grandmere stood up on unsteady feet. "Walk with me to the back yard. I'll show you the herb garden."

A new awareness came to Razelle as she realized how much her precious Mamie had aged since she'd seen her last.

She reached over and slipped an arm around her shoulders.

"We'd love to see your garden." Razelle walked with her Mamie out the patio door to the backyard that was filled with row and rows of greenery. Luke walked beside them.

His eyes widened as he looked at the luscious vegetable garden.

She giggled at the look on his face. "Amazing isn't it? So many rows of vegetables and herbs."

Luke nodded, taking it all in and not saying much. He was getting a better glimpse into his wife and he liked what he saw.

"Here we are. This was Razelle's favorite place as a child. She learned quickly the names of the herbs and vegetables in our garden." Grandmere pointed out the different herbs.

The older woman spoke from memory. "This one is cornflower used to help chest pains resulting from colds and to control fever. This next one, is Hawthorne berry which when ground for tea, helps to relieve coughing. These lilac leaves when placed fresh on wounds, draws out infections. If you dry the leaves, you can make them into a tea to help ease a cough."

Grandmere continued on down the rows of herbs, pointing out each one and how they helped when a person was sick from a specific ailment.

"Mamie, it always amazed me how much you knew about all these herbs. Do you still bring your herbs and vegetables to villagers?" Razelle couldn't help but be curious about Mamie's life since she'd last seen her.

They stopped at the last green shrub in the herb garden and Grandmere turned to her. "Yes. I still take herbs and vegetables, especially to villagers who are sick. Sometimes people stop by asking if I have something that will help cure this or that." Mamie gave her a honey sweetened smile. "Just like I know you're doing."

"Now, I can see where Razelle gets her compassion and how she has learned so much about the healing properties of herbs." Luke leaned down to smell a bush of wild thyme.

Razelle nodded. "It's true Mamie. Without you teaching me all those years ago, there would be something big missing from my life. It's stuck with me."

Grandmere's eyes filled with unshed tears. "Oh ma cherie. You make me cry with such words."

"They're only the truth Mamie." Razelle turned to hug the older woman who she loved so much.

They spent the rest of the evening with Grandmere enjoying fish, herbed rice and fresh vegetables.

Later in the evening as they stood up ready to go back to their cabin, Grandmere asked. "Will you come visit before you go back home?"

"Of course." Razelle reached over to hug her. "I love you Mamie. Be back in a few days."

After saying their goodbyes, Razelle walked with Luke toward their water villa.

"Happy to see your Grandmere again?" He threaded his fingers through hers as if it was the most natural thing in the world. He looked her way and Razelle could hear the tenderness in his tone of voice.

Warmth filled her. "It was so good to see her. It was good to hear her voice. To hug her again." Her lips turned up at the corners in a happy smile. "And here I thought she was upset with me."

"Well she never got any of the letters you wrote."

Razelle shook her head, troubled. "I will need to ask Mother what happened to them."

"That's a good idea. But we don't need to worry about that now. For tonight, let's relax and enjoy ourselves." Luke squeezed her hand as they started down the wood dock that led to their water villa.

Raz was trying and losing the battle to calm her over active imagination. She imagined all sorts of reasons why her letters never reached Grandmere and none of them were good.

Was there more going on with Mother than she knew?

Fear gnawed at her nerves.

She needed to do as Luke suggested and let it go, at least for tonight.

Luke squeezed her hand again and Raz turned, offering him a slight smile.

Her eyes darted from the king size bed back to Luke, a slight frown on her forehead.

He grinned and held his hand up. "Don't worry I remember our agreement. This is the only cabin that was left and it only had one bed." He looked at the bed and then around the room. "I can grab a blanket and pillow and sleep on the floor if that would make you more comfortable?"

Razelle wanted to agree to his idea, but guilt stabbed her conscience. The floor would be terribly uncomfortable and this was supposed to be a relaxing vacation for them both.

She shook her head. "No, that won't be necessary. Maybe we'll just keep a rolled up blanket between us in the middle of the bed. That way we each can sleep in comfort and still stick to what we agreed on."

"Sounds good, Raz." Luke's warm smile and reassuring words helped erase the anxiety that filled her belly. He looked out the patio window into the dark night sky.

"It looks like we missed the sunset, but we'll try to catch it tomorrow night. That's okay. We should do something different tonight. Maybe we could watch a movie together before we go to sleep. Good idea?"

"Sure, I'd like that." That idea was the best one yet. That way she could focus on the movie, and not have to constantly stare at the handsome man who was now her husband.

"Before we do that, I'd like to shower and change." Razelle looked at the open bathroom that was without a door, and used her nervous hands to tuck her hair behind her ears.

"I'll close the curtains and go outside on the deck. Let me know when you're ready to see that movie." Luke tossed her his rogue smile and winked before he walked out onto the deck.

Razelle hurried through the shower and slipped into her pyjama t-shirt and bottoms.

Finally, she opened the patio door to the deck. "I've finished, Luke. I can wait out here while you shower."

"Sure. I'll be quick." True to his word, not ten minutes later, Luke opened the patio door.

He wore black sweat pants and a navy blue Seahawks t-shirt. Thick muscles rippled through the sleeves whenever his arms moved.

She couldn't help but appreciate the sight. Her gaze

locked with his and she quickly looked away. *What are you doing staring at him like that?*

Heat shot up her neck to her cheeks and she hurried inside.

Luke closed the patio door and pulled the curtains across the window.

Razelle grabbed a throw blanket from the sofa and wrapped it around her shoulders.

"Chilly?" Luke picked up the remote for the TV, but his eyes were on her. His rogue smile was back. It was almost as if he enjoyed seeing her uncomfortable.

"A little." Razelle realized her cheeks must still be bright red. She tried to think of how she could switch his focus away from her. "So what type of movie would you like to see?"

Plopping on the right side of the king sized bed she wrapped herself in one of the throw blankets from the sofa.

Combing through the ends of her long hair, she listened as Luke clicked the remote and rambled off movie titles.

"Action and Adventure?" Luke asked as the show he'd chosen came on the TV screen.

Razelle looked at it and nodded. "Sure. That sounds good."

Luke grabbed a bowl and poured a bag of popcorn into it.

He stretched his legs out on the other side of the bed.

The movie began and Razelle continued to comb through her hair.

Luke turned to watch her try to comb out a particularly difficult twist in her hair. "Let me comb your hair. I promise to be gentle."

"Um… sure. If you want to." No one had offered to comb her hair because they wanted to before. Mother had done her hair until she was old enough to take care of it herself, which was when she turned six years of age.

As her hair grew longer, it took a lot more time to comb it out properly.

She sighed as Luke's gentle fingers ran the comb through her hair.

"Am I hurting you?"

"Not in the least. This feels good. Thank you for doing this." Razelle sighed.

Luke shifted on the bed until his thigh brushed against hers.

His fingers gently sifted through her hair. It felt heavenly.

"Your long hair is so beautiful. It feels like silk in my hands." Luke whispered as he pulled the comb through her thick auburn hair once again.

It didn't take him long to comb through all of her hair.

When he finished the last strand she sighed and leaned back.

Thinking she was leaning against the headboard, she was surprised to feel Luke's chest against her back. "I'm sorry Luke. I'll move…"

"No don't be sorry. In fact, I was thinking this is perfect." He shifted his legs so they were on either side of hers. His arms wrapped around her, pulling her close and his lips brushed against the top of her head. "Your hair smells so good, sweetheart."

Razelle yawned as her body relaxed against the hard wall of his chest.

Her last thought was how she loved Luke's arms wrapped around her. She wished this night would last forever.

❦

LUKE LEANED DOWN, smelling the sweet flowery scent of Raz's hair. He kissed the top of her head and savored this moment with her.

His wife's long hair that hung past her waist, now laid spread across both his thighs like auburn waves of silk.

Raz was so beautiful inside and out.

Today as he heard her Grandmere talk about her childhood, he realized how much he didn't know about her.

What he learned, gave him a glimpse into both the happy and painful sides of her childhood.

There was also something strange going on with her Mother. Why would her Mother not mail the letters Razelle wrote as a child? Why would she not want her only daughter to write to the Grandmere who loved her so much?

These were questions they needed answers to. He didn't want Razelle to experience any more hurt or pain.

It was time she had someone to protect her. It was time she had someone to care for her. Someone like him.

He was her husband.

Well, he was her fake husband.

A furrow formed between his brows.

Admit it man, you've gone and developed feelings for your fake wife. You're falling for her. That wasn't part of the deal. Now what are you going to do?

As he ran his fingers gently over Raz's forehead, for the first time Luke realized he was in far deeper than he bargained. But, from the way his feelings had grown for her, he wasn't sure he wanted a way out.

If anything, he wanted to dig his heels in deeper and get to know his new wife better than ever.

CHAPTER NINE

uke

"It looks like we're almost to the top of Magic Mountain." Luke stopped on the narrow path and looked behind him.

Razelle's breaths came in short and fast, her cheeks were stained red and perspiration glistened on her forehead.

She was a wonder.

They had spent the last five days exploring the island, and having fun. This honeymoon-vacation had been the best time he'd ever had.

He was reluctant for this time with her to end.

He'd woken up this morning — as he had the previous four mornings — with his arm around his wife.

He must have crossed the boundary line of the rolled

up blanket sometime in the middle of the night. He got up before she woke, removing himself from the temptation of wanting to kiss her soundly.

After a quick cold shower, he got dressed and went to sit on the deck enjoying a cup of coffee while he waited for her.

She had joined him an hour later and when he'd suggested they hike up the mountain this morning, she'd agreed.

Raz stopped with a hand on her hip and sighed in weariness. "Oh I hope so, Luke. I can't remember ever hiking this mountain as a child. I'm so tired."

"I know. We'll make it to the top together." He grabbed her hand and together they walked the last few steps to the top of the mountain.

A gate-like fence surrounded the top of the mountain, so that visitors wouldn't accidentally slide down on the other side.

"This is paradise." Razelle's eyes widened as she surveyed the three hundred and sixty-five degree view they had of Moorea Island.

"Stunning. You can see the brilliant blue ocean water that meets the blue of the sky. Which makes it seem like the ocean and skyline never ends." Luke mused. From this high up they could see everything.

"We're on top of the world. It feels like there's more freedom when we're up this high." Razelle twirled a little, giggling as she turned around and around.

Luke pulled out his smartphone and began snapping pictures of her having fun.

"Hey what are you doing?"

"Capturing the moment. You're beautiful like this."

"Thank you Luke." Stepped next to him and he pulled her further into his embrace. He slipped a finger under her chin, lifting her face up to his.

"I've never seen you so carefree and happy. This is the real you. You've captivated me." Luke leaned down and gently placed his lips over hers. The strawberry taste from the fruit they shared this morning, lingered on her lips.

He embraced her more fully, delving deeper into her mouth. It was only when he heard a quiet whimper that he stopped.

Stepping back for a second, he was surprised to see tears streaming down her cheeks. "What's wrong?"

With his thumb, Luke wiped the tears from her cheeks.

Looking into her bright green eyes, he waited for her to speak.

"Nothing… I mean everything." She sobbed again, quickly wiping the tears from her cheeks. Luke reached for, wrapping his arms around her.

After a little while Raz calmed enough to speak. Her voice wobbled as she explained. "Being with you on top of this mountain is so freeing. I think I'm just now beginning to realize how much I've missed."

She swallowed back emotions. "When you said at long last I look carefree and happy, it hit me that the last time I remember being carefree and truly happy was when I was living here with Mamie."

"In all the years since then, my life has become more confining with endless cycles of isolation." Raz expelled a shaky breath. "I long for what I'm feeling right now to last forever. I desperately need this — this freedom to be me. To be who I truly am."

She swallowed and wiped away more tears.

"Has it always been that way with your Mother?" Suddenly he needed to know more about her.

"Not when I was a child. But, when we moved back to the States, Mother became more watchful of me. She put more restrictions around what I could or could not do."

"Around that time, was when she began to punish me by forcing me to stay in the house for weeks on end." Razelle sighed heavily. "At the beginning I thought she was simply overprotective but since visiting GrandMere, I can't help but wonder if there's some other reason for her fear."

"Maybe there is." The furrow in his brow deepened as he thought of the possibilities. None of them were good.

"I don't know what reason she would have to fear anyone. She's always been so strong. She's always been convinced everything she did was the right thing. And she's always been the one to tell me what I'm doing wrong so I can be a better person too." Wrapping her arms around herself almost in a protective stance.

"A better person? What do you mean she told you what you were doing wrong?" Luke couldn't imagine that there was much that Razelle did that was wrong.

She swallowed quickly and Luke could see the pain of past memories reflected in her haunted green eyes. "I realize she was trying to make me a better person, but sometimes the words Mother used were hurtful."

"Go on." His body tensed, waiting in expectation of another dreadful revelation.

Razelle turned to look out at the ocean beside them. "Sometimes she would tell me that I didn't work hard enough to show my gratefulness for all she did for me."

His wife put a shaky hand behind her ear. "And there were a few times when she assured me, the way I looked — with my freckles and wide eyebrows and green eyes — was homely and unattractive."

"She doubted that any man would want a girl like me. But she told me, I didn't need to worry because I could just live with her for the rest of my life."

A lone tear ran down her cheek and she swallowed convulsively.

"I hope you know that's not true?" Suddenly it was important for him to hear her answer. Had she been brainwashed by her Mother to believe she was ugly or not good enough?

She looked up at him and her eyes held unshed tears captive. "I don't know. I always believed it to be true. My own Mother wouldn't lie to me, would she? Yet, since being here and talking to Mamie, I'm starting to think there might be many things I believed that might not be true."

"Well, in this case, what your Mother told you isn't true. You are not only beautiful, but you are compassionate and altogether good." Luke wrapped gentle fingers around her upper arms and squeezed lightly, as if to say — please believe me.

A shallow smile surfaced and her hands fidgeted with the golden butterfly that hung on the gold chain around her neck.

She stepped back from him. "Thank you, Luke. It means so much to hear you say so."

She exhaled slowly and she looked down at her feet, shifting slightly. "I think I just want more freedom. I want to learn what it means to live normally — in an un-caged world — like my friends."

Luke permitted himself a quiet smile, rather than scare her with his anger at her Mother's words and actions. "Well, now you're with me. Your Mother can't hurt you or lock you in a cage any longer."

As she looked up at him once more, her hollow eyes spoke of gripping anxiety that seeped into disappointment and shame.

One look at the pain etched plainly on Raz's tormented face and Luke's anger dissolved.

He moved suddenly to shorten the distance between them.

Luke liked having her close to him.

He loved kissing her and holding her. However, the fascination he felt for her wasn't merely physical.

It was much more than that.

Something buried deep within her had reached out and touched something deep within him, something profound.

Luke's inner self had connected with hers.

After his own pain and heartache from being rejected by love and feeling the hopelessness and loneliness that went with it, Luke could understand what his new wife was going through in a deeper way that she imagined.

With Razelle he experienced a feeling of wholeness, a rightness that had been missing from his life.

"I'm sorry you went through all of that." Luke groaned as he reached for her, folding her in his arms. "I promise to do everything I can, so you can have the freedom to be you."

At first her body was stiff and unmoving, resisting his comfort. But Luke held her close to his heart because he couldn't bear to let her go.

His hands cupped her face and Luke directed her mouth to his, kissing her again and again until she relaxed and slipped her arms around his neck.

Luke heard her breath quicken and he knew he'd reached her.

※

RAZ'S HEART seemed to stop and time stood still as Luke pressed his lips to her.

He had just listened to her ramble on about her Mother and all about her struggles with feeling alone and unworthy her entire life.

It was humiliating.

Her husband must be thoroughly disgusted from listening to her sob story by now.

Yet, if the heat of his kisses were any indication, he didn't seem repelled by her.

She made one last attempt to move away, so he couldn't kiss her further.

But he pulled her so close to him that could feel the outline of his hard body against hers.

His kisses deepened and her limbs melted like hot wax against him.

Her heart beat faster and she could scarcely breathe past the wild pounding of her heart.

She shouldn't have told him so much about her past. She wasn't even sure why she'd done it, other than the fact that she wanted him to somehow bridge the gap between their lives.

He was her husband after all. And she desperately wanted for them to be closer. She only had a couple other friends in her life. But, deep down she was aware that Luke's friendship would be deeper and require more from her.

She knew that, because she was already falling for him.

She couldn't let that happen. She didn't think she would be able to survive it, if he rejected her.

No, she needed to learn to guard her heart.

Foolishly, she had shared more about her past than she should have.

Surely now Luke saw her as she was... unworthy and much too scarred for him to be anything more than his fake wife.

She eased herself away from him, out of his arms.

"I... I think we should stop." Raz whispered, already erecting the walls around her soft heart.

Luke grabbed her hands, as if not wanting to sever their connection. "I'm sorry, I got carried away. You're right." He kissed the back of her hands.

The warmth of his lips against her skin caused a tingling up her arms. She quickly pulled her hands away.

"Well, we could go one last time to visit your Grand-mere. After all, we did promise to go back."

Razelle nodded. "Yes, I'd like that."

"Before we go, I hope you don't object to one last picture together?" Luke put his arm around her so the background of the photo overlooked the spectacular scenery of the Island and the boundless ocean behind them.

"Of course not." She forced a smile, despite the fact that her emotions were a mess.

He took more than one picture of them together, telling her he was trying to get the perfect shot.

Finally, Luke had got all the pictures he wanted. Grabbing her hand, they walked down the mountain.

They passed plenty of hikers coming up the mountain as they went down it. She was glad Luke had asked her to go in the morning, as it would've been too crowded this afternoon.

It was almost late afternoon by the time they arrived at Grandmere's home.

She answered the door immediately, almost as if she expected their visit.

"You two look tired. Sit down there in the shade. I'll bring you something cool to drink."

"Mamie, you don't have to go to any trouble on our account." Razelle could see she was moving around slower today. "Here, I'll help."

Grandmere reached into the fridge and pulled out a large pitcher of peach juice. Raz found three glasses in the cupboard and placed them on the small island in the middle of the kitchen.

"You have chosen well, ma petite Cherie." Mamie spoke softly as she poured the juice into the glasses.

"What do you mean, Mamie?"

"You've chosen a good husband. He treats you well." Her eyes glittered with meaning. "He loves you."

Three simple words, yet her Mamie didn't realize how untrue her assumptions were.

Yet, she couldn't really explain that theirs was a fake marriage. "He doesn't know all there is to know about me yet. When he does, I'm very sure any love he has for me will fade away."

Grandmere shook her head silently, a knowing smile on her lips. "Non, ma Cherie. Then you don't see what I see. His love for you is strong. I've been watching. Your husband's eyes follow wherever you go and he looks at you as a priceless jewel."

Razelle was certain her Mamie was seeing things. "We'll see." She didn't know what else to say to her Grandmere's confident words.

"Would you let your old Mamie give you a word of advice, ma petite Cherie?" One look at Mamie's sober face and Razelle nodded quickly.

"Of course, Mamie. I would appreciate any advice you give me."

Grandmere's voice was low, almost conspiratorial. "Don't push your husband away because you're afraid. Instead talk to him and let him discover the real you. He will love you for sharing yourself with him and your love will grow."

"I'm not so sure." Razelle was uncertain that Mamie's advice would be helpful with Luke.

"Let me tell you a story." She nodded, waiting. "My husband and I were married for nine wonderful years before he passed away, God rest his soul. But, that first year was the hardest."

A faraway look came to her eyes. "My husband Teanu was always doing things for me, but I pushed him away. Deep inside I didn't think I deserved his love or any of the kindness he would show me."

"One day he said to me, if you really don't love me Leilani just say so. We can go our separate ways. You won't be bothered by me anymore." Grandmere shook her head and looked down to her wrinkled hands.

"His words shook me to my core. It only took me a few seconds before I finally told him the truth: *I love you, but I don't feel like I deserve your love.*"

"Oh, Mamie." Razelle couldn't imagine anyone who deserved love more than her Grandmere.

"It's true. But then you know what, my husband told me I did deserve love and he was going to keep proving it to me for the rest of his life. And he did."

"Mamie, that's a beautiful story. Teanu must have been a very loving husband to you." Razelle sighed heavily. In her mind, that kind of love was just a dream.

"Yes he was. I still miss him everyday. But you can have that too with Luke. Let him get to know the real you. He loves you already. But then his love for you will only grow, I promise." Grandmere reached over and touched her cheek gently with a wrinkled hand. Suddenly it felt like she was four again, receiving the love of her Grandmother.

"I will try, that's all I can promise."

"Good. Now let's go find your Luke." She carried the drinks to the deck, to see Luke relaxing in the chair under the shade of the tree. Mamie followed behind and they enjoyed a nice quiet chat together.

When it was time to leave, Luke hugged Mamie, but Razelle clung to her. "Thank you for everything. I will write to you, okay?"

"Ah, ma cherie. I will love to hear from you and will cherish your letters." Grandmere hugged her once more. They were just about to leave when Mamie reached out and touched her necklace.

"I see you still wear the butterfly key. Do you still listen to the music box?" Razelle's hand lightly touched her butterfly necklace, remembering when Mamie had given her the gift. She translated for Luke.

"It's a key?" Curious, Luke lifted the golden butterfly to see that it really was shaped like a key. "What does it open?"

"A music box that Grandmere gave me for my birthday when I was five years old. It played the song *you are my sunshine*. I remember when I was little, listening to it everyday for hours on end."

Her lips formed a gentle smile. "I was always reminded that Mamie told me the butterfly was to remind me that I was growing from a caterpillar and stretching into a beautiful butterfly that would have the freedom to fly when I grew up."

Razelle forced a smile passed the sadness that wanted to overwhelm her.

Mamie asked. "You still have the music box?"

"No." Razelle swallowed, hoping her Mamie wouldn't ask any more questions.

"What happened to it?" It looked like it was a day for telling the hard truth.

Her tone wriggled between frustration and anger. "My Mother threw it against the wall on the morning she found out I had been going to the homeless camp. It's my fault. I was the one that snuck out at night, without telling her I was going." She swallowed back tears and her voice came out high and strangled.

"I'm sorry Mamie. It broke in pieces. I really loved that music box, because it was from you."

Grandmere shook her head from side to side, her lips making a clicking sound. Memories came back of Mamie making that sound when she was upset or worried.

"It's okay about the music box. It's not as important as you are. And you are still that butterfly, you don't need the music box for that." Grandmere cupped her face with both of her hands, brown eyes searching hers. "I worry for you. Stay close to Luke, he will protect you and I will keep praying."

Razelle's throat constricted and she swallowed back tears. "Thanks Mamie. I appreciate you."

"Now you get home safely and don't forget to write to me." Mamie's big smile along with her embrace was like a blanket of comfort.

Grandmere stood at the door and waved as they walked away. Razelle blew her a kiss, a few tears still streaming down her face.

She would miss her. Raz decided she would write as soon as she got home.

❧

Luke slipped his arm around Razelle and pulled her close to his side. "It will be okay."

He hated to see her like this.

And after all that he heard, he decided it was more important than ever to protect his wife from her Mother.

Right now however, she needed cheering up.

"I planned a wonderful dinner tonight at the Lagoon Resort outdoor restaurant if you're up for it? I hear the food is good and the view is incredible. Might be a nice way to spend our last evening here."

"That would be nice Luke." Tears shimmered on her eyelashes as she looked at him. "It would be wonderful to do something to relax and have a little fun. Thank you for thinking of it."

Luke nodded.

He hoped that all this trouble would simply blow over for Razelle, but deep inside he had a feeling that the storm was just beginning to rise… for both of them.

Could they weather the storm together?

A spark of determination rose up from the inside.

He would do everything possible so they could make it through this, closer than ever.

azelle

"I'M GLAD YOU TEXTED. It's been way too long since we talked." Cassie walked toward Raz carrying her favorite hot drink, a chai tea latte.

"It's been much too long. Come sit down beside me." Razelle patted the space beside her on the old wooden bridge that overlooked the wide river that ran into Paradise Lake.

Cassie sat down, swinging her legs over the side of the thick wood beams. "I never understood why you liked coming to this out-of-the-way bridge."

She just shook her head as she stared at her friend. "All you have to do is look at the view. The sky is a beautiful pink and blue and you can listen to the flowing river and watch as it catches up with the lake. It's beautiful and very peaceful here."

Cassie took a sip of her hot drink, as she looked around her. "You're right. It does have a certain natural appeal."

Razelle grinned. "It sure does. But, it still isn't as beautiful as Moorea Island."

"Do tell." Cassie flicked her eyebrows in a suggestive manner. "I've been itching to hear all about your honeymoon with Luke."

"It was good. And it was a vacation not a honeymoon." She grinned when her friend rolled her eyes.

"It was too good, maybe." Razelle reflected on the almost perfect time she had with Luke on the Island.

"Too good? How could anything be too good?" Cassie shook her head in disbelief. "Now, you have to tell me. It's been three days since you flew home and I've been waiting for the details."

Razelle laughed out loud. Cassie was so dramatic sometimes. But that was one of the things she loved most about her friend.

"All right, all right. I'll tell you." Raz grinned as she remembered her time with Luke. "We stayed in one of the overwater bungalows that overlooked the ocean. And there was even one time when we had an authentic French Polynesian breakfast when they brought breakfast to us by canoe."

"No way. That must have been amazing." Cassie's eyes widened with a gleam of wonder.

"It was." Razelle went on to describe their visit to Coco Beach and swimming with stingrays and sharks.

"I'd be scared. They didn't attack you?"

"No. The guides know what they're doing. We were relatively safe. And it was incredible to watch those sea creatures in their natural habitat under the ocean." She told her about seeing Grandmere.

"Mamie told me, she didn't receive any of those letters I wrote when I was seven." Raz shook her head in unbelief.

Cassie nodded. "I can't say I'm surprised."

"What do you mean?"

"Well, I'm sure you must realize your Mother has tried to control you for years. Either through guilt or by force." A steely anger was reflected in Cassie's eyes.

"I realize at the time you were just a child, but now you're an adult. And you don't have to put up with her games anymore."

Razelle nodded her agreement. "I know." And she did, but there was still a part of her that felt a loyalty towards the woman who raised her.

"I'm so glad you were able to see your Grandmere."

"Thanks Cassie. It was wonderful." Razelle could still feel Mamie's arms wrapped around her. "I promised I'd write."

"Good. She will love that." Cassie looked over at her. "So, you introduced her to Luke?"

"Yes. Mamie liked him, but I'm not surprised." Razelle thought back to their conversation in the kitchen. "Mamie told me that Luke loved me. She said she could see it in the way he looked at me."

"Wow. That must have been some honeymoon."

Razelle smiled. "Again, it wasn't a honeymoon. It was a vacation. We have a fake marriage, remember?"

"Whatever you want to call it." Cassie waved her hand imperiously in the air. "Do you think your Grandmere has the right idea?"

"No, I don't." Heat stained her cheeks as she thought of their movie nights together and their hike up Magic Mountain.

"Okay I can tell there's more that you're not telling me. Spill." Cassie leaned her arm on the railing, and leaned closer.

Raz knew her friend wasn't going to let her get away until she'd told her all the important details.

"Cassie, you wouldn't believe how nice Luke was to me this whole vacation." Memories came back, filling her with a warmth in her belly at the thought of their time together.

She told her friend about walking the sandy beaches in the hot sun and about their hike up Magic Mountain.

"I shared with him how I'd felt unattractive and unworthy all my life and how I longed for more freedom. He assured me I was beautiful and that he would do everything he could to protect me from being hurt by my Mother again."

Raz paused, heat penetrating her cheeks. "Then Luke kissed me. Kissing him is like waking up under the sun. Warm and right." Razelle sighed. "Problem is, now I feel more attracted to Luke than I ever did."

"Problem? That's not a problem. It sounds to me like you've been thoroughly kissed and wooed by your husband. That's truly terrible." Cassie tossed her a breezy smile.

"Fake husband, remember?" To Raz's mind, those words made all the difference.

Cassie gave her head a little shake and took another sip of coffee. "Okay spill. What is it exactly about your relationship with Luke that's got you worried?"

"Well, our fake relationship didn't seem so fake to me during this week vacation. Luke treated me so well. He bought me fun clothes and gifts, made sure we had one of the nicest villas to stay at on the water and took to the beach and great restaurants." Sweet memories of their time together filled her with warmth all over.

"He did it all, including listening to me talk about how unworthy I've felt. He got a deeper glimpse into my heart and I feel like we've become much closer now." Razelle sighed heavily. "To tell you the truth, it has scared me so much that since we got back home, I've started to back away from getting closer to him."

Her lips tightened and her shoulders drooped slightly as anxious thoughts returned.

Cassie leaned closer to her. "Look at me, Raz."

Razelle lifted her gaze to stare into her friend's blue eyes that at this moment were serious, in a tone that said she'd brook-no-interruption.

"Raz, listen to me. I know you're afraid. Heaven knows, I would be too if I was going through the same thing. But, I really believe you need to give Luke a chance." She leaned in closer. "You said yourself, he's treated you so well. Why not give this relationship a chance and see where it goes? You might be surprised."

"Oh Cassie." Razelle shook her head. Her friend just didn't understand. "Don't you see? This marriage isn't real. That was our agreement." Raz's voice wobbled and she swallowed back her fears. "We agreed to stay married for one year. He'd get his great-grandfather's land and I'd get the money and then we agreed to go our separate ways. It wasn't supposed to be this hard. We had a plan of how this was supposed to go. There wasn't supposed to be any hurt feelings when all was said and done."

Her friend chuckled softly, shaking her head. "Raz, it seems like you're trying to tick all the correct boxes of a financial statement. Since when does any relationship go according to plan?"

Raz shrugged, aware of the truth of Cassie's words. "I know, I know. You're right. Marriage relationships aren't easy. But, it's the closeness of this marriage relationship with Luke that worries me. How will I be able to put a stop to this attraction I have for Luke and get through these next eleven and a half months without falling head over heels in love with him?"

"Maybe you don't put a stop to it. Maybe your Grand-mere was right when she said Luke loves you." Cassie whispered. "Maybe you're not the only one who is struggling with their feelings. What if it's true and Luke really is falling for you?"

Raz silently shook her head. How could this perfect man really and truly fall for someone like her? "No, he's too perfect. He's a billionaire who also happens to have a supportive and wonderful family. He's a man who does what's right, no matter what and he takes care of those he loves."

Razelle shook her head firmly. "No, I really don't think Luke's been waiting to fall in love with someone like me."

"Why not?"

"Let's see. I am as poor as a church mouse and I have a Mother who is super controlling who borders on psychotic. Not to mention that I have so many things I don't like about myself, that I'm a bit of a mess myself. How could Luke not like all of this?" Razelle waved her arm, encircling her whole body in the statement.

"Raz, those lies your Mother has fed you all these years have warped your thinking." Cassie clucked her lips in disapproval, shaking her head.

"I truly believe Luke isn't going to care about how much money you have or don't have, he'll protect you from your Mother. All those flaws you say you have, that's in your head. I don't believe Luke sees any of them as flaws. From what I can tell, Luke has been passionately wooing you."

"Sometimes it seems that way, but since we flew home and for the last three days, Luke has really kept his distance. I definitely feel like I've been getting mixed signals." Razelle ran a hand through her hair, expelling a heavy sigh.

"Is it possible that you and Luke have been giving each other mixed signals? Maybe instead of running away from each other, you need to begin talking again." Cassie's matter-of-fact tone and her street-wise words steadied Razelle.

Still, she wasn't quite ready. Desperately she looked for an excuse. "Luke's gone so much. In fact as soon as we got back, he began working again at his Seattle office. He's been there from dawn to late evening for the last three days."

"So what? You two live in the same house, Raz. Find time to talk to Luke." Cassie leaned ever closer, punctuating her words with a rat-tat-tat sound like that of gunfire.

Raz reluctantly nodded, admitting defeat. "You're right. I'm just scared. But, I know I need to stop letting fear make choices for me." She paused and in a subdued voice said. "I'll talk to him."

All too soon, their chat was over. Razelle hugged her friend. "Thank you."

"Call or text me. Let me know how things go." Cassie hugged her once more before walking away.

Razelle began to walk home, her thoughts returning once more to Luke.

Somehow she would find the courage to push past her fears of rejection and fear of intimacy and get to know her husband better.

Luke's face came to mind and a longing for him to be her real husband gripped her. She wanted him to be her husband in every sense of the word.

Luke stared at the computer screen like he had been for the last thirty minutes.

His usual enthusiasm for working on updates to his budgeting software just wasn't there today.

And he knew the reason.

Razelle.

Ever since they had returned from their week together, she had distanced herself from him.

But, if he were being honest, he'd backed away too.

Whatever closeness he had gained with his wife during those incredible seven days together, had faded away like a beautiful memory.

They'd been dancing around each other for days now.

Remembering their time together, Luke realized the problems had started on that last day on Moorea Island.

They'd gained a new awareness of each other on top of the mountain. For the first time, he felt like he was really getting to know the real Razelle.

And that kiss. It was incredible and had given him a reason to remember the name of the place where he'd felt a seemingly impossible closeness to his wife, at Magic Mountain.

His wife was more than he'd even hoped for. She was compassionate, funny, beautiful and perfect for him.

He had savored their kiss and their closeness, but suddenly something had changed.

After their visit with Raz's Grandmere, his wife suddenly retreated. It was like she stepped away from him, to a place deep inside herself that he didn't know how to reach.

She had gone from being his fun wife who was laughing and playing freely to being a woman who was somber and melancholy all in a matter of minutes.

Leaning back in his chair, Luke tried to piece together what had gone wrong.

Was it when Razelle told Grandmere of her Mother wrecking her music box that had caused the change?

Whatever the reason, he didn't know how to reach her.

Which was one of the reasons he had also distanced himself from his wife. It was also the reason he'd spent so much time at work ever since they arrived back home three days ago.

Luke stood to his feet and began pacing. Thoughts of Razelle continued to trouble him as he stared out at the view from his large office on the top floor of Stevenson Be Safe Development Corporation.

Luke needed help gaining the right perspective.

With a sigh, he reached for his desk phone and buzzed his receptionist. "Mrs. Sanderson, would you ask Jack if he has a spare moment to meet me in my office?"

"Of course, sir."

Lost in thought, Luke didn't even hear the office door quietly open and close.

"You're pacing. You hardly ever pace." Jack's voice was low as he walked across the office. His brother sat on the corner of Luke's desk, picking up the framed photo nearby.

He gave a head nod to the picture in his hand. "What or should I say who has got you all tied up in knots?"

Luke had framed the picture he'd taken of him and Razelle on top of Magic Mountain. He'd wanted to remember how that day had been for the two of them.

He sighed softly. This was most definitely his big brother. "That's what I like about you Jack. You cut to the chase."

Jack shrugged and set the picture down. "I figure the sooner we get straight the point, the sooner we can fix it."

"You're right." Luke turned away from the window and

ran a hand through his hair. He walked to his mini-fridge and grabbed a couple of bottled waters, tossing Jack one.

Opening the drink, Jack took a long drink of the cool clear liquid. "So, is it your wife that has you all in a bother?"

"Yeah." Luke took a drink and then explained about their wonderful vacation on Moorea Island. "We were just beginning to get so much closer, connecting on a deeper level, when she began to pull away."

"Tell me what happened."

Luke sighed and began. "We went to one of the highest and best mountains on the Island, Magic Mountain. We shared a beautiful kiss and I felt Raz was really opening up to me. I told her that I'd never seen her this carefree and happy."

He ran a hand through his hair as he remembered. "Suddenly, she was sobbing. She told me that the last time she felt truly free was when she lived on that island with her Grandmere."

"I felt like she had a real breakthrough as she realized how abusive her Mother has been. She told me what she truly wanted was freedom to be herself and to be loved for who she was. That's when I took that picture."

A small smile turned up the corners of Luke's mouth as memories surfaced of that day. "After we went down the mountain we went to her Grandmother's house. Raz and her Mamie talked for a while in the kitchen, we had drinks and said our goodbyes."

"Right before we left, Raz's Grandmere asked her what happened to the music box. My wife seemed broken explaining that it was her Mother that wrecked it. But

Jack, I can't understand why she keeps taking the blame for all of this."

Jack's brows puckered in concern.

"Later that evening we ate at this beautiful restaurant, but by that time, my wife had begun to create more distance between us." Luke rubbed the back of his neck and shook his head.

Jack nodded, silent for a moment before he spoke. "Sounds like she's had it rough. If painful memories have been coming up in her life, it would explain why she's distanced herself from you, Luke."

"Yeah, that makes sense."

"It sounds like your wife has been hurt once too many times by her handlers in the past and now she's like a skittish horse who tries to bolt at the first touch of someone new." Jack drank the rest of his water.

As he set down the water bottle Jack's intense gaze focused on Luke. "You'll need to show her everyday you love her."

"I didn't say..." Luke began, when his brother interrupted.

"Please, I could tell the moment you started talking about your wife that you love her." Jack stood to his feet, throwing his water bottle in the recycling bin.

"It won't be easy, but you'll need to be patient with her, Luke. Keep being kind and love her, even if she sometimes frightens away. You'll need to be persistent to woo her until you win her heart completely."

Luke pressed his lips together and nodded, thanking his brother on a whoosh of expelled air. "You might just have the best set of street-smarts around Jack. Dad used to say you had good horse sense. At any rate, you've got it and I appreciate you tossing some of that wisdom my way."

"Anytime, little brother." Jack grinned and grabbed him into a quick hug.

As Jack walked toward the door, Luke's phone buzzed and Mrs. Sanderson's voice spoke crisply. "Mr. Stevenson, Christina from downstairs reception says there's a woman in the lobby who insists on speaking with you. She told me to warn you that she's quite upset and keeps waving a magazine around. She thinks it has a picture of you?"

"Thank you Mrs. Sanderson. I'll be right there."

Jack raised his eyebrows as he opened the office door. "Better you than me. Hope it goes well. Let me know if you need backup." His brother winked and clicked the door shut.

Luke couldn't think of any clients who had called or emailed to say they were angry with him. And what was that about a picture in a magazine?

Over the past few years, since he and his brothers had become successful, there had been many times when his face was seen in a magazine somewhere.

He wasn't going to spend time worrying about it.

Slipping on his suit jacket, he hurried to the elevator to the first floor lobby determined to deal with the problem quickly.

As the elevator doors opened, his heart nearly stopped.

Standing in front of Christina the receptionist — waving an open magazine — was his wife's Mother.

"Do you hear me? This is insulting!"

From her loud outburst, Luke knew he'd caught her in the middle of an angry rant.

"Ms. Chattaine? I was told you were here to see me?" Luke did his best to keep his tone calm. Maybe by doing so, he'd help bring peace to this situation.

"Yes. I most certainly am here to see you Luke Stevenson." Angelique Chattaine walked toward him with the determination of a bulldozer ready to flatten him. Her high heels clicked a staccato rhythm on the marble floor and her brown eyes flashed with fire.

"What can I do for you?" Luke held his gaze steady with hers, and waited.

"You can tell me what this is all about." She held up one of Seattle's most popular society magazines. The pages opened to a large picture of him with his arm around Razelle in her wedding dress. Someone must have snuck onto his property and used a telephoto lens to take the photo.

"Your daughter and I were married a little over a week ago." He wasn't about to tell her it was a fake marriage.

"And this is how I find out about it? From a magazine?" She looked around the room at other clients who were now openly staring at them. Luke grimaced.

Razelle's mother was obviously milking this scene for all it was worth. Her Mother continued. "Why would you do this to me — her own mother?"

"I'm sorry we surprised you. But from what I gathered, my wife was tired of being locked up in her room and wanted her freedom. We grew to care for each other quickly and decided to get married. That's all I can tell you." Luke's words were calm and reasonable.

"I did not lock her up. She needed to be disciplined, so she was cut off from contact with her friends. Obviously I hadn't counted on you going against my wishes." Her voice was high and shrill.

"Your daughter is a twenty-one year old adult. She is a caring and compassionate grown woman who deserves respect to make her own decisions even if they aren't in agreement with yours." Luke's voice was stern and he could feel the heat of anger burn in his veins.

"She is my daughter. I get to tell her what she can and cannot do. Not you." Her voice screeched higher. "You took my daughter. You stole her from me. You're a thief and a liar and a daughter-stealer. I hope you burn for what you've done to me. You will regret this! I promise you!"

Razelle's mother definitely had a temper and it wasn't pretty to see. It was definitely time for her to leave. Luke had had enough. "I think you're in no mood to talk about this reasonably and I've heard enough. I want you to get off my property, or I will call security and have you forcibly removed."

With one last heated glare, Angelique Chattaine turned on her heels and left the building.

As soon as the doors closed behind her, he smiled at everyone who was still watching. "Everything is fine." He spoke in calm even tones and before long the people were back to reading their magazines or clicking on their Smartphones.

His heart rate was still too fast by the time he got back to his office.

Knowing he wouldn't be able to concentrate any more today, he decided to take Jack's advice and talk to his wife.

Besides, since he'd just talked to her irate Mother, there was no telling if she'd come after Raz next.

He would go home and talk to her.

He would do everything possible to protect his wife... even if it had to be from her own Mother.

CHAPTER ELEVEN

uke

As the cabin came into view, Luke breathed out long and slow.

Driving up the gravel road that led to Grand's cabin — his cabin now — had always given him a sense of calm even when things were topsy-turvy around him.

Much like they had been today.

Ever since Raz's mother had unloaded her anger on him earlier, a swirling mixture of emotions began an uncomfortable churning in his belly.

He needed to talk with his wife. He needed to explain what happened.

Luke wasn't sure of his wife's feelings toward him. All he knew was he wanted to get closer to her.

Remembering Jack's advice, he realized he needed to be kind and to keep being patient with her.

He could do that.

Parking the truck near the cabin, Luke stepped out and saw Razelle.

Thick auburn hair was tied up in a loose ponytail that hung down her back. She was wearing a green t-shirt and jean shorts. She was kneeling down in the dirt plucking out weeds.

She looked beautiful even with dirt up her arms.

Luke couldn't believe the woman in front of him had agreed to be his fake wife. He was beginning to care for her in a way that made him really want to exchange the fake marriage and make it real.

He hadn't cared for his ex-fiance as much as he was beginning to care for his wife. Audra had been fickle, evidenced by the way she'd suddenly left him at the altar. Razelle on the other hand was faithful and willing to stick with him.

He respected the fact that in spite of the tough decision to leave her Mother and all that was familiar, she'd done it anyway. Ever since childhood, his wife hadn't had it easy.

He hoped that by marrying him, that somehow he could make her life better. Maybe he could even help bring some happiness to her life.

All of a sudden, guilt pricked his conscience. He'd been much too distant ever since they got back from Moorea Island. How was she supposed to be happier if he didn't make time to talk or be with her?

It was time for him to make some changes.

Luke thought of the surprise he had scheduled for early afternoon. Maybe that would cheer her.

He walked to where she knelt in the dirt.

Crouching down, he playfully bumped her shoulder with his own.

"Luke." Surprised, she dropped the gardening tool in her hand. Wiping stray hair back from her cheek, she rubbed a little spot of dirt onto her cheek.

Scanning her facial feature with the freckles on her nose and now the smudge of dirt, Luke thought he'd never seen anyone more adorable. "You're adorable especially with the little smudge of dirt."

A red stain coloured her cheeks, like the blossoming of a rose.

Touching a finger lightly to her cheek, Luke nudged the dirt off her face. He stared at her slightly longer than usual, getting lost in her emerald green eyes.

"Thanks." She whispered and looked down for a moment, dark brown lashes lightly dusting high cheek-bones. Her hands fidgeted with her gardening tools, gathering them together. "You came home early." It was a statement, but her voice was hesitant and questioning.

"Yeah. There was an incident that happened at work. I found I couldn't focus anymore, so I decided to come back home." Luke grimaced remembering.

A pucker formed between his wife's brows. "What kind of incident?"

Luke paused a little before answering. How did he tell his wife about what happened today? "Your Mother stopped by unexpectedly."

"Oh no." Raz dropped her tools and stood to her feet. "What did she say?"

"She waved one of Seattle's society magazines in front of my face. It seems a reporter must have found out about our impromptu wedding and captured us in all our finery." Luke did his best to keep his tone light, so as not to burden his wife.

Razelle shifted on her feet. "So she knows. I'm sure she said more than that. Mother has never been able to keep quiet when she's upset."

"Yes. She was quite expressive in her disapproval of our marriage." Luke did his best to keep his expression neutral so as not to upset his wife.

A troubled expression grew on her face. "Did she threaten you?"

"She simply let me know I'd regret it." Luke shortened the distance between them and he cupped her chin, peering into his wife's troubled eyes. "There's nothing to worry about. I'm sure she was just venting her anger at being taken by surprise by your wedding."

"I wouldn't be so sure. Mother's anger can be a scary thing." Her whispered words came out pained and her breathing became uneven and shallow. It was almost like she was reliving her own nightmare.

"Hey, I'll do whatever it takes to protect us both, don't worry." Luke placed his forehead against hers and ran his hands gently up and down her shaking arms. After a few minutes his wife's breathing returned to normal and the shaking in her body lessened.

"You okay?" Luke stepped back slightly so he could see her face.

She nodded, wiping a stray tear from her cheek. "Yeah. Just thinking about my Mother makes me either a scared shaking mess or it makes me so angry I can't speak."

"I'm sorry."

"Me too." Her solemn eyes met his. "I mean it. I'm so sorry she came to your office and lashed out at you because you chose to marry me. I'll go talk to my Mother and tell her to stop bothering us."

"No."

"Why not?"

Luke sighed heavily. "I think it's much better if you don't talk to her. When I think about how your Mother reacted to the news of our marriage and combine that with the little pieces you've shared with me of your childhood, I believe it would be best if you stayed away from her."

He paused. "At least stay away from her for now. Maybe if you give her time to get used to the idea, she'll see reason."

"I'm not sure time will help, but I'll stay away from her because you asked me to." His wife assured him.

"Thank you. I appreciate it." Luke breathed a little easier. He was worried that if his wife confronted her Mother, the situation would only get worse. If his chat with Angelique Chattaine earlier was any indication, she wasn't about to see reason about her daughter's marriage to him, any time soon.

Razelle bent down and picked up her gardening tools. "I'll go put these away and then…"

A loud rumble from a truck engine interrupted their conversation.

Stepping close so Raz could hear him, he whispered. "Don't put those tools away quite yet. Here comes my surprise."

"What surprise?"

Luke waved for her to follow him. He directed the truck to the large space behind the cabin. Before long two men got out of the truck and unloaded a rototiller, some top soil and some gardening tools. The men got to work quickly digging up a large patch of ground.

"Luke, what are they doing?" Razelle hurried behind him and grabbed his arm to get his attention.

He grinned. "I'm giving you a garden for your birthday present."

"But my birthday isn't for a week."

Luke grinned. "I know. But when I saw you on the Island, looking so happy in Mamie's garden, I realized you needed a vegetable and herb garden of you own."

Her green eyes grew large, shining as bright as the smile that lit up her face.

"Oh Luke, thank you." Razelle threw her arms around his neck. "You don't know how I've longed for my own garden."

He held her close, savoring the moment. Seeing her happy was far better than the haunted look in her eyes earlier.

They men turned off the rototiller. Razelle pushed on his chest and reluctantly Luke loosened his tight embrace.

He wished his wife could have stayed in his arms much longer.

❧

Razelle stepped away from Luke and with a shaky hand pushed back a tendril of hair.

Embarrassed by the way she had practically thrown herself into her husband's arms, she tried to divert his attention to something else.

"Looks like they finished getting the ground ready for the garden." She watched the two men as they packed up their equipment and with a wave they were gone.

"Looks like it. Ready to get to work?" She nodded, excited to begin planting. Luke hurried over to the shed behind the cabin. He'd only been gone a couple minutes, when he walked out carrying a large wooden box.

Curious she followed him. When he set down the box, she saw it was full of seeds of all kinds. They were all labelled, so she could find which ones she wanted easily enough.

"Luke, you have enough seeds here for three large gardens. And so much variety too." Happily she flipped through the many packets of seeds finding the ones she wanted to get started with.

"I hope that will be a good start."

"It is. This is more than enough." Razelle stood to her feet with both hands filled to the brim with packets of seeds.

She looked over at Luke. "Will you bring a couple buckets of water? Oh, and can you double check the water is warm, not cold?"

She'd learned the hard way that using cold water when she planted her seeds in the soil, caused her plants to think it was winter, which made them go dormant.

"Sure, I can do that." While Luke filled up water buckets, Razelle grabbed a string and some stakes from the supply of things Luke had brought out of the shed. It didn't take long before she had lined up a dozen rows, ready for planting.

"I'll plant some vegetables first. I'll need to cut potatoes and I'll plant those in a few days, so I'll save a row for them. But, today we can plant carrots, peas, lettuce in these rows and the last few rows we'll keep for herbs." She was so excited she could stop chattering.

"I also saved a separate patch to plant strawberries and a row for a few raspberry bushes." Razelle happily got busy organizing her seeds along the rows, so she remembered where she wanted to put each one.

They worked the land, planting the seeds and watering it.

Using a large water pot that drizzled water gently over the rows they'd planted. Razelle had just finished watering the last row, when she saw Luke walking toward her carrying the rest of the bucket of water in his hands.

"Oh good. I'm glad you've got water." She looked at her hands, pants and shirt that were caked with dirt. "I thought I might wash…"

She didn't even get a chance to finish her sentence before Luke splashed her face and the front of her shirt with water.

"Is this what you need?" Her husband grinned, enjoying himself a little too much.

"Hey, what are you doing?" Soaked through, she decided there was no way she was going to be the only one wet.

Two could play at this game.

"Now you're going to get it." There weren't any more buckets of water, but all of a sudden she spotted the garden hose.

Hurrying toward it, she turned on the nozzle, grabbed the water hose and began to chase him.

She managed to catch up with Luke when they reached the far end of the garden. She put her finger on the end of the hose, making the spray of water wide.

It wasn't long before the spray of water reached his whole body.

Razelle giggled.

"You've soaked me all the way through. But, since I'm soaked anyway…" Luke made a mad dash for the garden hose. There was no way Razelle was going to give up so easily. She clung to the hose with all her might, weaving it in the air like a sword. But Luke had other ideas.

Chuckling, he grabbed her, placing one arm around her waist and with his other hand he tried to wrangle the hose away from her.

She tried to move out of his grasp and tripped landing on the ground.

Luke hung on to the garden hose and went down landing with most of his weight on his elbows and knees.

"It's mine." Even though she wanted to win this contest of wills, Razelle could tell her hand was weakening. Luke's grip was so much stronger than hers.

Peering at him through wet lashes, she tried one last time to yank the hose out of his hand. Instead of gaining control, Luke pulled it out of her hand.

He held the hose just to the side of her body.

His brown eyes glittered with mischief. "Do you cry uncle?"

"No way." Razelle wasn't sure what made her decide to be stubborn this late in the game.

Luke suddenly sprung the water hose and stuffed it behind her neck down her shirt.

"Oh… that's so terribly cold." Her teeth chattered, her whole body shivering. "I can't take it anymore, Luke. I cry Uncle!"

Mercifully, her husband pulled the very cold garden hose away from her frozen body and threw it far away from them.

"You're so cold." Luke looked down at her, a rogue smile covering his face. "I'm sorry for all that cold water. Forgive me?"

She smiled. "I should make it tough on you first… but I won't. I forgive you."

"Then, let me warm you."

Her eyes met his for a timeless second.

From the way her husband's eyes darkened as his gaze met hers and looked down at her lips, she knew he was about to kiss her.

Just as she knew she would welcome his kisses.

Her body went numb, tingling with wonder and anticipation.

HE COULD TELL by the stillness of her body that she felt shaken, much like he was.

Luke slid a thumb across her bottom lip, his eyes

pensive. "I've never experienced anything like this, like what I feel when I'm with you."

It was important that she knew what he was feeling was as much as a shock to him as he could tell it was to her.

He hadn't expected this to happen. In fact since his ex-fiance had deserted him, he had avoided getting close to any woman.

He'd only thought of the fact that he needed a fake wife to receive his inheritance. He never would have imagined that this woman would dominate his dreams, and his every waking moment.

She was everything his unspoken dreams had been about a future wife and a thousand things more.

"Me either." Her green valley eyes were filled with innocent wonder.

He stared at her lips for a long moment and his mouth inched toward hers.

Her accelerated heartbeats echoed his own and Luke leaned closer.

His wife put her hands around his neck slowly and deliberately. She tilted her face up to receive his kiss.

They were so close, her skin buzzed with anticipation.

He gently lowered his lips to hers, his lips firm and tender. Their mouths softly moved together and it was the sweetest sensation he had ever experienced.

Luke groaned and buried his face in the curve of her neck. "You taste so very sweet."

His breaths came out rapid and uneven.

Luke pulled away just for a moment and when he saw the small smile on her face, he reached for her again.

His wife's arms tightened around his neck, pulling him willingly toward her.

Then Luke's lips met hers once more, twisting, tasting, testing, feeling the need to return and re-experience these sensations. He felt the need to convince himself that they were real.

Razelle trembled in his arms.

He looked at her and saw that her face was unnaturally pale.

"You're cold. Let's get you inside and warm you up." Luke pulled himself to a standing position and held out his hands to help her up.

Placing his arm around her waist, he walked to turn off the water hose, before hurrying into their cabin.

He kissed her forehead. "You go ahead and change into something dry and warm and I'll get the wood started in the fireplace. Bring me your wet clothes and I'll put them in the dryer."

His wife headed to her bedroom, while Luke started a fire and added wood. As he brought in an armload of wood from outside, he couldn't stop thinking about Razelle.

With the fire burning brightly in the background, Luke heated the kettle to boil.

Finding two mugs he stirred in the hot chocolate mix, looking forward to spending a little more time with his wife.

As he turned his head, he saw her.

She stood there in figure-hugging jeans and a warm yellow sweater looking incredibly beautiful after her shower.

Razelle's thick auburn hair was still wet and hung past her waist like a shimmering veil in the firelight of the cabin.

Luke swallowed, standing silent and unmoving, drinking all of her in.

"Luke, are you all right?" She said quietly and moved towards him.

He nodded. "Just thinking about how incredibly lucky I am to have you in my life."

"I feel the same way about you. But…" There was hesitation in her voice.

"No, buts." Luke spoke firmly. "Tonight, we don't need to go through the list of what we agreed on or why we might be wrong for each other."

He continued. "For tonight, I would like us simply to get to know each other better and enjoy each other's company. What do you say?" Luke didn't want to be reminded of their fake marriage agreement.

They had so much fun today and he wanted it to last forever. But he'd take what he could get.

"Sounds good. I think I smell hot chocolate."

Luke grinned and turned, picking up both mugs. "Get comfortable by the fireplace and I'll bring your mug."

They settled in on the love seat nearest the fireplace and sipped their hot chocolate, enjoying watching the flames leap from one piece of wood to the other.

Razelle settled on the cushioned sofa with her feet pulled up to her side. "The smell of wood burning like that of a campfire, has always been a pleasant memory for me. I'm not sure why, because I don't remember Mother and I going camping or even doing anything in our backyard."

"Maybe you had campfires with your Mamie?"

"No we didn't." Razelle shook her head a line forming between her brows. "I don't know what it is about campfires, but anyway I'm so grateful you got the fireplace going tonight."

"The best part is that I get to sit beside you." Luke winked pleased when he saw her cheeks turn pink.

"Thanks Luke." She was silent for a few moments before she turned to him again. "I really love this cabin. You've done a great job restoring it."

"Thanks. It was fun. With each job I took on from the floors to the walls, to rebuilding the kitchen, I wanted it to be restored to how it must have been back in Grand's time when he bought the land and built this cabin."

He looked around the cabin. "Of course, I added a few new amenities, like washer and dryer and a new fridge, but the structure of the cabin itself is renovated as close to the original design as possible."

"It looks great."

Luke looked around the room, enjoying the fresh cedar on the walls and the new wood smell that permeated the cabin.

"It was a fun project to work on. Doing everything myself, made me feel a closer connection to my great-grandfather. I know that sounds strange." He rubbed the back of his neck, feeling somewhat uncomfortable sharing something that had touched him deeply.

"Please, I'd like to hear more about when you were a boy. What do you remember about coming here with your Great-Grandfather?" Razelle settled more comfortably resting her head against the couch's cushion and offering him an encouraging smile.

"All right. Coming here as a young boy, filled my head with wonder and many dreams." Luke began to go back in time. "I remember Grand loved coming here for the early part of the summer each year. He had a big head of cattle and some horses on this land. I dreamed of being a cowboy, and running this ranch someday."

A grin lifted her lips. "Of course."

He smiled. "But that wasn't the only fun part. Since Grand's land is also connected to the waterfront along Paradise Lake, it was the perfect place to come and enjoy farming life, but also have access to the water.

"Sometimes, he would take me to go body boarding and body surfing when the weather was good for it." A warmth spread thought his body as he remembered. "Grand would often talk about how he wanted to build a sprawling ranch house and also continue to operate a large cattle operation. He was passionate about everything he did."

"I think you've inherited his passion."

"I did. But as a little boy, I was just happy that I could spend time with Grand. I loved riding horses and chasing cattle just like he did. We were a couple of cowboys."

Raz had a curious look on her face. "What about the oil derricks I saw on the back end of the property?"

"Those three oil derricks are what makes this land pay for itself and it would pay for the cattle too, if I had any." Luke rubbed the back of his neck as he thought about it.

"I've been thinking of building a large ranch house and

buying more cattle and turning this place into more of a ranch. What do you think of that idea?"

She lifted her eyebrows in surprise. "I'm surprised you would even ask me Luke. That's totally your decision."

"But I would really like to know your thoughts on that Razelle. I respect your ideas." He really did want to know her ideas on this.

But it wasn't simply because he respected her. He pushed the thought aside for now that deep down he was hoping she would stay as his real wife.

She smiled and spoke softly. "I think Luke, that seeing what you did with this cabin, any ranch house you built would be simply amazing. As for turning this place into a cattle ranch, I think it's a great idea. You'd have a chance to live your dream."

Luke nodded and smiled. "I would." He really wanted to tell her that the dream would only be complete if she was here with him as his wife.

They both finished sipping their hot chocolate and placed their mugs on the coffee table.

Razelle leaned her head back on the softly cushioned sofa. He could tell her eyes were starting to droop a little.

He was surprised when she spoke again. "Luke you're so kind, thoughtful and handsome. Why haven't you married? Well, before me I mean?"

"I was engaged to a woman once." He paused, not wanting to think about his ex-fiance.

Razelle turned to him, her green eyes soft with compassion. "What happened?"

"I was barely twenty-one years old. I'd gone to Texas and started working as a roustabout for Boone Donovan's oil company. You met Hudson at the camp… Boone's his dad. Anyway, Hud and I started there together right out of high school. Somehow I managed to talk Hud's dad into hiring me."

"He took a chance on me as a scrawny kid who didn't know anything about working in the oil patch or about leading people. But, by the time I was there two years I was leading men and managing crews." Luke raised his eyebrows slightly, still surprised at Boone's belief in him back then.

"I'm not surprised. You're a great leader, Luke." Razelle softly spoken words carried a weight of belief that floated down and settled in his heart.

A man could live a lifetime trying to please a woman who believed in him like that.

"I'm grateful you think so."

"But, back to your story. It's just getting interesting, I think."

He grinned and turned on the sofa, so he could see her a little better. "It was around that time I met Audra, who was the head of public relations for Donovan Oil."

"She was pretty and after a while I asked her out." Luke's brow's puckered as memories returned. "We started dating and getting to know each other. By the time I'd been there three years, I'd asked her to marry me."

"She ended up not showing up to the wedding, leaving me at the altar with no bride and no wedding. I've never been more disillusioned, angry or humiliated." Luke expelled a breath, as if by breathing out he could rid himself of the memories of that horrible day.

"I'm so sorry Luke. That's awful." Razelle spoke quietly.

Her soft words connected to him on a deep level. "It was awful."

Raz's eyes glistened with moisture and a few tears trailed down her cheeks. "I'm sorry to hear about your ex-fiance. Sounds like there were many difficult things she was dealing with."

Razelle turned to look at him. "But I'm also sorry that you had to go through that kind of pain and rejection. I have a little bit of personal knowledge of how terrible it is to feel rejected and unloved."

His fingers gently wiped a stray tear from her cheek.

"I know you understand in a very real way." Luke had never known a woman as compassionate as his wife. She had suffered so much and still felt things deeply when others were hurting.

Razelle silently shook her head. "Your ex-fiance didn't see the real Luke Stevenson that was about to make his dreams come true and make his Great Grandfather proud. You are a great catch for any woman, Luke. Don't you forget that."

With half-lidded eyes, she looked at him with a gentle smile on her lips. She closed her eyes, and leaned her head on his shoulder, curling up to him.

He kissed the top of his wife's head and his brows puckered in worry as troubled thoughts plagued him. His wife didn't know that he felt a big responsibility toward what happened to Audra.

Looking down at the Raz's angelic appearance as she slept, Luke realized someday soon he would need to tell his wife the real reason they could never have a real marriage.

Shifting on the sofa, he lifted her, carrying her in his arms to her bedroom.

After laying her on the bed, he sighed deeply as he covered her with the blanket. Leaning over he kissed her forehead and grazed her lips.

One thing was for sure, now he was more convinced than ever that his feelings for his wife went far beyond simply being attracted to her.

He loved her.

But she could never be his.

A man like he was, who hadn't seen the signs that his ex-fiance was struggling, didn't deserve a real marriage.

A man like him didn't deserve to be loved by a beautiful woman like Razelle.

CHAPTER TWELVE

azelle

RAZELLE STEPPED out of the shower, toweling herself off as fast as she could go.

She'd forgotten that today she was to have brunch with Luke's Mom, Grandmom, Rory, Bella and Elle.

Eliza Stevenson had invited her to join the Stevenson women for brunch and shopping a few days ago.

Luke's note along with his credit card on the kitchen counter this morning had jarred her memory: *Good morning, beautiful. I really didn't want to go to the office today, but wanted to spend the day with you instead. Thank you for yesterday. You were in my dreams. I'll see you tonight.*

Then her husband had added: *p.s. Don't forget Mom is picking you up for Brunch this morning. Take this credit card and don't be shy about buying whatever you need. Mom's driver will drop you off at my condo in the city. I'll see you later. Yours, Luke.*

Warm tingles spread from her belly up to her heart when she read his note. He'd signed his note, yours.

After the wonderful day they had together yesterday, she could think of nothing she wanted more than to be his real wife.

Raz sighed heavily. He was so thoughtful to encourage her to buy what she needed too. Even though she realized Luke was wealthy, it didn't make the gesture any less kind.

As she thought of buying an evening dress and the accessories she would need for tonight's charity ball, she realized more than ever that she didn't even fit into his world.

Luke deserved a woman that was better, more cultured and more worldly-wise than her.

All she'd ever done was live in different places with her Mother and work in a coffee shop in the poor side of town. She only had a few friends and definitely didn't even have the right kind of clothes for his world.

Her emotions swirled with a mixture of confusion of where she fit in Luke's life and frustration at her lack in so many areas.

Shaking it off, she determined to make the best of things. This wasn't a real marriage anyway, which meant it shouldn't matter.

But somehow, she couldn't convince herself of that.

Deep down, some part of her wanted to please her husband and his family, even though all they had was a fake marriage.

As she searched through her meager assortment of

clothes, she found a black pair of dress pants and sand cream colored blouse.

These clothes were a few years old, but they were the best she had and they would have to do.

Standing in front of the full-length mirror in her bedroom, she combed out her long hair and quickly gathered it into a braid.

Looking at her reflection with her green eyes and lightly freckled nose, she frowned. Her red-brown hair seemed to highlight the freckles. She remembered her Mother saying her freckles made her look unsightly and plain.

She sighed. There were some things she simply couldn't change about herself.

They would have to accept her as she was.

Just as she was adding finishing touches to her makeup, she heard a loud knock on the door.

Opening the door she saw Eliza Stevenson with a gentle smile on her face.

She reached over and pulled Razelle into a gentle hug. "I'm so happy you're coming with us today. I've been looking forward to getting to know you better."

"Thanks Mrs. Stevenson." She whispered.

"Please, I would love it if you'd call me Mom, dear." Eliza took a step back, blue eyes shining with warmth.

Her eyes pricked with tears and she nodded. "I'd love that, Mom." Trying on the word, she felt its warmth as it slipped off her tongue.

A peaceful calm and a sense of love and comfort settled on her. The feeling that she was accepted and loved for who she really was. The sensation was new and she was a little awed by it. Was this what being close to a Mom was supposed to feel like?

Luke's mom put her arm around her shoulders. "I do too."

Razelle savored the feeling. The last time she remembered feeling the gentle touch of a mother figure was when Mamie had hugged her.

Throughout her childhood and as she'd grown up, not once did she have a memory of her Mother embracing her.

As a little girl, whenever she'd hurt herself, her mother would wave her hand to shoo her away and tell her to stop crying.

She soon realized not to go to her Mother when she was in pain. Instead, she turned to cuddling her cat Sunbeam or to dig her hands in the dirt, helping to cultivate life in something else.

Messy emotions threatened to spill over as she got into the car. Feelings she believed were long buried rose up like bile in her mouth. She swallowed them back.

She glanced at Luke's mom, thankful that she did most of the talking as Eliza's driver drove them to Seattle. Her driver dropped them off, near Fisherman's Wharf.

"Thank you Henry. I'll text you when we need you later on." Eliza spoke to the driver as he opened the car door for them.

"Of course. I'll be waiting, Mrs. Stevenson." Henry nodded and got into the car and drove away.

As she followed Eliza into the Sandpiper restaurant, Razelle began to feel a little intimidated.

She had only driven past this restaurant a few times

with her Mother, but they'd never stopped. She'd been told that despite the fact that the restaurant was known for it's wonderful seafood, it also boasted exorbitant prices. The message was clear that eating at the Sandpiper was outside the realm of their meager budget.

Despite feeling out of her league, Razelle was happy to finally have a chance to enjoy the food at this restaurant.

Eliza chatted with the maitre d' like he was an old friend and soon they were ushered to a table in the corner. Rory, Bella, Elle and Luke's Grandmom were waiting for them as they sat down.

"Razelle, so nice to see you again my dear. I'm glad you could join us today." Catherine Stevenson reached over and squeezed her hand, a generous smile on her lips.

"Thank you. I'm glad to be here." Razelle went around the table saying hello to Rory, Bella and Elle who were enthusiastic in welcoming her with warm embraces and soft kisses to her cheek.

Razelle glanced around where they were seated. She appreciated how the room's lighting combined with its rich wood and thick dark red carpet, created a sense of intimacy and warmth that was very appealing.

She toyed with the napkin by her plate, a sense of nervousness nearly overwhelming her.

"Don't worry, it takes a little getting used to going to restaurants like this." Rory whispered in her ear. Some of the tension left Razelle at those words. She knew Rory from her growing up years and despite the fact that she'd married Gabe Stevenson and was now a rich woman, Rory still remained humble and a good friend.

"Thanks." Razelle sighed. "I needed to hear that."

"Well ladies, should we place our orders? The food here is delicious. Order whatever you would like to try." Eliza Stevenson sent a happy smile to all the women around the table. Soon the waiter came and took their orders.

When her seafood Caesar salad arrived, it was piled high with shrimp, crab and scallops. They all had some type of seafood for lunch along with a shared bottle of wine.

They talked among themselves between bites.

"This is perfect. I feel like my stomach is finally getting the food it's craved for so long." Eliza patted her hand. "What about you my dear? Are you enjoying your meal?"

Razelle smiled happily, turning toward her. "Yes, it's great. I think I could get used to this."

Eliza chuckled gently. "Well, we'll need to do this again then. What do you think Rory, Bella, Elle?"

"I'm definitely coming back. This is perfect and so nice to have Jack at home taking care of our son." Bella sighed contentedly. "It won't be long before I'll have baby number two to take care of, so I'm enjoying the short amount of time I have to get away for an afternoon."

"That's how I feel with our two small children. I'm enjoying this time away relaxing like this." Elle looked over at her. "You might feel the same way Razelle, once you have your first baby."

Heat caused her cheeks to blossom pink. "You might be right." She was so not ready for the topic of babies, but she hoped they wouldn't see that Elle's words flustered her. Luke and her were in a marriage-of-convenience, but most likely Elle didn't know that.

If someone would have asked her yesterday, she would have said if Luke's kisses were any indication there was hope that their fake marriage would become a real marriage after all. She had even dreamed of his kisses last night and had woken up feeling happy that Luke was opening up to her.

Remembering Luke's note from this morning, a flutter of happiness swirled in her belly.

However, now that she was getting a taste of Luke's world of abundance, Razelle wasn't sure she would ever fit in.

A seed of doubt sprang up like a weed in her mind, trying to drown out all the wonderful things that had already happened in her life because of marrying Luke.

Razelle just hoped she could get through this year of her fake marriage without experiencing too much pain and heartache at the end of it.

"Well, I for one am ready to go shopping. How about you girls?" Luke's Grandmom's glanced at everyone around the table.

"More than ready." Elle spoke and the other women laughed and shared their agreement.

After Eliza paid the cheque for the meal, she stood to her feet. "You know girls, I'd like to take the long way around and walk along the pier with my newest daughter-in-law. That is, if Razelle agrees?"

She nodded in her direction. "Of course."

"Then it's settled. We'll meet you on Pine Street." Eliza grinned, leading the way out of the restaurant. When they got to the Pier, she looped her arm through Razelle's.

Luke's mom began talking, her voice kind. "So tell me

how you've liked living in that cabin on Luke's Great-Grandfather's ranch land?"

"I like it there. It's nice and quiet, with nature surrounding us everyday." Razelle breathed out slowly thinking of their peaceful spot. "I love nature and plants. Luke and I even planted our own garden yesterday."

"That's so good. I'm sure you'll enjoy the fresh vegetables. I enjoy my small garden too. That's another thing we have in common." She grinned, bumping Raz's shoulder playfully.

"I'm glad." It felt good to have one thing in common with Luke's Mom, besides Luke himself.

"Do you know, Luke has told me that he thinks you are an amazing woman. My son deeply admires and respects you."

"Luke said that?" Her husband didn't say all that much. For him to praise her to his Mom, well that really meant a lot to her.

Eliza nodded. "Certainly. It seems whenever I talk to Luke lately, he's always mentioning little things he admires about you. I can tell by the way his tone of voice softens when he talks about you, that you are really special to him."

Even with Luke's sweet kisses yesterday, in the back of her mind she always came back to their agreement. Theirs was a marriage based on convenience, not love.

He had made it clear from the start, and it's what she had agreed to. Yet, despite what they'd agreed on, Razelle couldn't help but be drawn to the Norman Rockwell type of picture Luke's mom painted of them as a young couple in love.

She wished it were true.

"My son has told me that you have a real talent for growing things like vegetables and herbs." Eliza whispered conspiratorially. "I can't wait to come back to the cabin sometime this summer and get a good look at your garden."

"Thanks. I love working with my hands in the soil and watching things grow. It's very soothing." Her compliment couldn't help but make Razelle smile.

Eliza looked out at the landscape around them silent for a moment. "Luke mentioned your beautiful trip to Moorea Island. You enjoyed it?"

"Yes. It was so relaxing and peaceful."

"I didn't realize that you lived there as a child."

Razelle paused for a moment, unsure how to begin. "Yes. Mother moved us there when I was three years old. Then while Mother worked in different restaurants, I lived most of the time at an older woman's house."

"She was someone I adopted as my Grandmother. I called her Mamie as a child, and well it stuck." Razelle smiled with warmth at the memories.

"How wonderful to have a Grandmother in your life who you can share all the important moments of your life with." Eliza's soft voice almost seemed nostalgic. "That's someone to treasure throughout your life."

"I know. I wrote her a letter as soon as I got home. Mamie said she'd write me back. I can't wait to hear from her." Razelle grinned, thrilled that her relationship with Mamie had been rekindled.

"I'm happy for you." Her blue eyes held a trace of moisture.

Razelle was comforted by Eliza's gentle presence.

"Luke also told me what a compassionate soul you are. You've been going with your friend to the homeless camp outside of Paradise Lake, bringing food and helping those who are sick."

"Yes, but it was originally my friend Cassie's idea. For almost a year we went there about once a week to help out. There's a man in charge of the camp, who is not very nice. I worry for the teenagers there." Razelle admitted.

"When I saw Luke's leg, I wondered what was going on." Eliza expelled a breath, sighing heavily. "But, I'm confident that both you and Luke will be able to help whoever needs it at the camp. I'm sure there are many teenagers grateful that you're there."

Guilt pricked her conscience. She hadn't been back to the camp, not since her Mother had banned her. Maybe now it was time to return. She wanted to see Addy and the other teenagers again.

"Thanks Mom. You've helped me to regain some needed perspective. Luke has also been a huge help to me. Your son is kind, compassionate and generous to a fault."

Eliza chuckled softly, nodding. "He is his father's son. Daniel was always helping others. Did you know that Luke's dad was the one who rescued me from a human-trafficking situation years ago?" Razelle's eyebrows shot up. "Not long after, Daniel asked me to marry him. The rest, as they say, is history."

"I'm sorry you went through that, but I'm happy Luke's dad rescued and married you." Razelle quietly thought their love story was quite romantic.

"Me too. They are bittersweet memories." Eliza turned to her, tears shimmering in her eyes.

"I think your son feels the same way."

Eliza nodded slowly. "Yes, he loved his Dad and was truly lost there for a few years. It really shook Luke up, when his Dad died. Our family struggled to make ends meet financially, and as a single mom with five boys we were devastated by his loss emotionally too."

"But, Luke was twelve years old at the time. He was at the point of figuring out who he really was. He got in with the wrong crowd. They called him names and bullied him and he began to hang out with teenagers who pushed drugs.

"For a few years there, I didn't know if we were ever going to get the real Luke back. He was a wild young teenager, unsure of his identity and where he fit in his own family or where he fit in the world around him." Eliza's voice softened as she told the story.

She continued. "One day a friend of Luke's nearly died from a drug overdose. He was really shaken up by the incident. Luke began to turn around for the better after that. As he focused on helping his friend Waylon get out of the drug crowd, Luke also helped him curb his reckless spending."

"Luke worked everyday to help Waylon overcome not only the addiction, but also the tendency to waste his money." Razelle could hear the glow of pride in Eliza's voice as she spoke of her son.

"Luke is responsible for helping Waylon find his way back to who he really is. To this day Hudson is his best friend and very loyal because of how Luke helped his younger brother."

"I can tell they have a very close bond. But wow, I didn't realize that about Luke." Raz pondered her words.

"Yes, Luke is very loyal and committed to protecting and helping those he loves." Luke's mom continued, speaking softly.

"He helped his ex-fiance Audra too. Luke told me later that the year that they were engaged, Audra's mood swings were terrible. He didn't realize it at the time, but she was bi-polar and on prescription medicine. Some days she was happy and other days, she was so depressed she didn't want to live."

Eliza shook her head sadly, remembering. "But Luke was loyal to her. I think he believed he could help her. But, she wanted a different life. She left Luke at the altar and soon after began dating Nate Caldwell who was an executive in Donovan Oil."

"But things didn't work out between Audra and Nate and they broke up. Only a week later, Audra overdosed on prescription drugs and died." Eliza sighed deeply.

"Luke was devastated. He moved back to Seattle, went to college and began working days and weeks on end to design his financial software, creating those apps, and ended up fixing that small cabin on Grand's ranch land."

Eliza's voice sounded sad. "I think ever since Audra's death, he's blamed himself. And because of that he has hidden himself away for years, believing he is better off alone."

"I'm sorry he's gone through so much heartache and pain." Razelle reached for Eliza's hand to give comfort.

Luke's mom released a gentle sigh. "He has. All that pain has made him too afraid to love. He's been too afraid of trusting another woman and misreading her motives. He's afraid of being hurt, so he pushes people away before he can be hurt by them."

Eliza stopped then and pulled Raz into a hug. "That's why I'm so glad he has you by his side to show him how to trust again. To show him how to love again."

Something in her tone made her ache for Luke. She had been pushing him away. She'd been the one who had been terrified by the power of her own feelings.

Maybe it was time for her to completely let down her walls and open up her heart to the possibility of loving her husband.

She squeezed Eliza's hand and they walked in silence until they reached the designer clothing stores.

"Now we'll go shopping for tonight." Eliza smiled brightly as they walked along the boulevard and began shopping at a store that had quite a collection of evening dresses.

Razelle followed Eliza down the aisle where the long evening gowns were on display. Her jaw widened as she looked at the prices. One dress cost two months wages.

While Rory, Bella and Elle looked in the other aisle, a woman who worked there came to help them.

"We're looking for a beautiful evening gown for my daughter-in-law. Could you show us some ideas of what you think would look good on her?" Eliza smiled at the associate and nodded at Razelle.

"Of course. Follow me to the very special dresses. There are a few there I think will be beautiful on her." The lady had a slight French accent and seemed to glide across the store.

As Razelle followed the woman's lead but she couldn't help but feel a little intimidated by all the luxury that surrounded her.

She'd never been in these high-end stores in her life. Being here in this store together with Luke's mom and her three sister-in-laws, made her realize how far apart their worlds really were.

The lady from the store carried a few dresses in her hand and at Eliza's nod, she was shown into a spacious dressing room.

Rory went outside the dressing room with each new dress she tried on.

It wasn't until the last one that Eliza gave her a big smile. "That deep emerald color looks beautiful on you Razelle. The beaded off-the-shoulder evening gown is a beautiful look on you, with your long auburn coloured hair. It hugs your slim figure perfectly. What do you think?"

"I've never worn something so beautiful. But, I do love it."

"Perfect. We'll take it." Eliza Stevenson spoke decisively to the associate who was eagerly waiting by the time Razelle slipped out of the dress and into her walking clothes.

Before long everyone had bought their evening dresses and the accessories they needed. Bella, Elle and Rory also helped Razelle find some wonderful designer shirts and pants in colors that enhanced her natural creamy complexion.

As soon as Eliza's driver picked them up they rested their heads back against the seats very tired from their full day.

Razelle was relieved when Henry dropped her off at Luke's condo. Walking in the door she soon realized he wasn't back yet.

She ached hearing Eliza talk about all the pain and heartache Luke had gone through.

She'd had a new awareness of why there were times Luke seemed to keep her at arms' length whenever things got too personal.

She really wanted to talk to him. She wanted to understand him and where she stood with him.

But he wasn't here.

Now, it looked like any conversation with her husband would need to wait until tonight.

"HEY LUKE."

"You made it back from Texas." Luke grabbed a virgin cocktail from a waiter carrying a platter of drinks.

"Yeah, just barely. Dad sent me there to check on things. Looks like he'll be promoting me to vice president in the next few weeks." Hudson shrugged, a half smile lighting the corners of his lips.

His friend was always the humble one. "That's really great Hud. You deserve it."

"But enough about me. How's your newest Budgeting app working out?" His best friend since High School had always been one of his biggest encouragers. Hud had continually asked about new projects or designs he worked on.

"We found a few kinks in it this week, so my team and I regrouped and are trying to solve the problem. Hopefully by next week it will be fixed and ready to present to the world." He grinned excited about the new software and apps they were using to help so many people with their finances.

"I'll be using it Luke. And so will many others. It's a good thing you're doing, but I'm not surprised." Hud reached his glass over and clinked Luke's half-empty one.

"Thanks man. It feels good."

"And how's married life?"

"Good. Raz is amazing." Luke nodded thinking of his beautiful wife who had disappeared with his mother as soon as she arrived tonight. He looked around trying to find her.

"Glad to hear it. Looks like your lovely wife is coming this way now. And I see my parents waving me over. Talk to you later." Hud nodded and walked away.

Luke didn't even notice his friend leave. He stared at the beautiful woman who walked toward him.

His wife wore an off-the-shoulder emerald evening gown. As she glided toward him, her long auburn hair swayed in a graceful rhythm with each step.

She was captivating.

He had returned to the condo only a few minutes before they needed to leave. He had spent the afternoon catching up with his brothers.

Then as his driver drove them to the benefit gala, he had been so texting with his team and dealing with the newest problems with the App that he'd all but forgotten about his wife.

However the biggest reason he'd kept busy was because of the fact that getting closer to his wife terrified him.

On some level, the intimacy that had begun with her during their week in Moorea Island had brought his deepest fears to the surface.

Luke had a whole new awareness that his new wife was chipping away at the walls he had carefully placed around his heart.

Tonight would be a balancing act. He would need to be a kind and thoughtful husband to her, and still guard his heart.

Seeing her like this, looking so beautifully angelic, made Luke realize even more she could never be his true wife.

"You look stunningly beautiful. Sorry I got caught up in yet another conversation and left you alone." He leaned close, kissing her cheek.

Large green eyes widened as Razelle's gaze lifted to his uncertainty in her eyes.

"I understand."

"Raz, can we talk later?"

"Sure." Tucking her hand under his arm, he led her toward a table near the stage where most of his family was seated with their hosts Boone and Millie Donovan.

"Razelle, you look beautiful." Eliza stood and kissed her on the cheek. "Let me introduce you to Boone and Millie Donovan."

His wife held out her hand as she greeted them. "Yes of

course. I do remember being at your house once before, under unusual circumstances." Smiling lightly she glanced at Luke. "It's good to see you again."

She smiled, nodding at his grandparents, mother and brothers and their wives. Luke could tell she was nervous. Sitting closer, he bumped his leg up against hers and squeezed her hand to reassure her.

They ate their meal together, mostly bantering back and forth. Luke sensed Raz wasn't her usual self tonight. Something was off. They would need to talk later.

Soon Boone Donovan made his way onto the stage. "We're here because we care about what goes on in our neighbourhoods, our state and our nation. We all want to give back."

"Many of us have had the privilege of aiding many causes like helping orphans and aiding the fight against poverty. However, at tonight's gala, the donations will be to help victims of human trafficking. Someone who has been in this fight is here to share with you his story. Please welcome a good friend of our family, Luke Stevenson."

"Thank you Boone." Luke shook his hand and stood behind the microphone. "You're here because you want to end human trafficking. I can tell you from experience, that it's a battle worth fighting."

He paused and looked over the large crowd gathered. Everyone was listening with rapt attention and it inspired him to tell his story.

Luke shook his head and paused looking over the crowded room. "Most of us have not been in that position where we are forced to do something because if we don't someone will harm our family. But I can tell you there are many children and teenagers and even some adults, who are forced to do just that."

He hesitated before continuing. "Even as we speak, I have a private investigator digging into a man who is suspected of being involved in not only human trafficking, but also in drug smuggling and other illegal activities. If they are found guilty, justice will be done."

"I think we all want more children and teenagers to be safely returned to their families or guardians once again. Because you have given to this important cause, many more people will be set free to live a normal and safe life."

Luke paused letting the importance of his words sink in. "Boone and Millie Donovan our hosts tonight, have decided that tonight's proceeds will go to Stevenson Be Safe foundation and the Safe House where we have helped many people who have been forced into slavery against their will, to get healthy so they can get back in society."

"My mom was a victim of human trafficking years ago, but my Dad helped rescue her." Luke smiled gently at his Mom. "My father has since passed away, but like my mom always tells us, she likes to imagine her husband looking down from heaven with a smile lighting his face tonight telling us, you've done well. And you have. Thank you for joining with us in supporting this cause."

Loud clapping began and people stood to their feet.

Luke stepped off the stage and walked toward his family's table. People shook his hand on the way back telling him that his words had helped them have greater compassion towards victims of human trafficking.

It seemed to have struck a chord with people at tonight's benefit, and for that he was grateful.

"You did good, son." Granddad squeezed his hand.

"These are proud tears, Luke." Grandmom had pulled out a tissue from her purse and was dabbing her eyes. Luke reached down to kiss her cheek.

"You always make me proud." His mom hugged him and kissed his cheek.

His brothers gave him good-natured fist bumps as he passed them walking toward his own seat at the table.

Luke slipped into the chair beside his wife and turned to her, reaching for his water glass.

Luke's hands fidgeted nervously while he waited to hear his wife's response. He was more nervous than he was to speak in front of a roomful of people.

"Your words touched a lot of people. I'm proud of you." Raz was pleased to be with Luke and it radiated off of her in waves as she smiled at him with pride.

"Thank you. I needed to hear that especially from you." Luke whispered in her ear, pleased when a blush stained her cheeks.

His mom and grandparents were talking with the Boone and Millie Donovan and his brothers and their wives were talking with each other.

"Glad you're doing something to get the bad guys, Luke." Waylon spoke up and swallowed his drink. Luke could tell from Waylon's white knuckled grip on his water glass, that it brought up old memories.

"It's what we've got to do, Waylon. We can't let them win."

Luke was about to continue talking, when Razelle's phone dinged with a text message.

After a few moments Razelle lifted her head before

leaning in to whisper. "Cassie told me she was at the camp last night. She said Addy has a black eye."

"Did she explain what happened?" Luke's brows shifted together and his lips formed a thin line.

Raz nodded, her eyes wide with concern. "Yes. Apparently Addy's friend Cindi had been taken by Sloane in the middle of the night and dragged out of their cabin. Addy tried to stop him and he punched her."

A tic formed in Luke's jaw.

"Cassie is asking me to come to the camp tonight. She wants the two of us to try and sneak Addy out of there." Razelle slipped her phone in her clutch purse, and looked back and forth between Hudson, Waylon and Luke.

Raz whispered. "I think I should help get Addy out of there. Addy can't stay there and be safe."

"You're right. She needs to get out of there." A chill slid over Luke and in that second a decision was made. "But there's no way you're going to the camp alone. I'm going with you."

Razelle nodded, a slight smile hovering over her mouth, almost as if she had expected nothing less.

azelle

LUKE AND HUDSON lay the oars down in the centre of the boat as it reached the shore on the other side of the river.

Razelle rubbed her sweaty hands along her jeans as she followed Cassie onto the rocky beach.

Fear nipped at her heels and she put a hand to belly to try to calm the nervous flutters there.

Quick footsteps crunching rocks sounded behind her. Glancing behind, Luke hurried to catch up with her.

As her husband approached, he settled his large hand on the small of her back. It was warm and soothing.

"Are you okay?" Luke whispered question carried concern. It was the reminder she needed that she wasn't alone.

She breathed out slowly. "Yeah. Only a little worried. I

just want to get Addy out of this horrible place without anyone getting hurt."

Her brows puckered as memories rushed in of Sloane and his men threatening them with their guns. Later on Sloane made good on his threat and shot Luke in the leg when he tried to save Addy.

Shaking her head, she closed her eyes and tried to calm her breathing.

"Hey. Look at me, sweetheart." Luke stopped her for a second and cupped her cheek with gentle fingers. "We will be right there with you. You might not see us in the shadows, but just know that Hudson, Waylon and I will be watching and waiting for any sign of trouble. We'll do whatever it takes to protect you."

Razelle nodded. The moon shone bright in the dark sky above and she could see his brown eyes shimmered with concern.

She smiled at his warm concern, her fears calming.

With Luke, Waylon and Hudson watching out for her and Cassie she reminded herself, they could do this. They must do this for Addy's sake.

"Okay. I'm ready." As she slipped a brave smile into place, Luke chuckled softly.

"You don't fool me for a second, but maybe this will help." Luke pulled her closer and with his fingers under her chin, tipped her head up.

Razelle's heart soared to her throat, beating wildly.

Gently Luke's mouth claimed hers. His kiss was tender. A kiss designed to erase her fears and calm her trembling body.

Except now she trembled even more, but not with fear.

No, now her body trembled to life in a slow awakening of desire for her husband.

"Luke, we can't do this now." She whispered and pulled away from him, burying her face in his strong neck. Her breaths were rapid and shallow and she forced herself to calm.

"I know." He chuckled softly and kissed the top of her head lightly. "But, did it help get your mind off your fears?"

"Yes." She nodded, glad for the dark cover of night, hoping Luke couldn't see the blush that stole up her neck to her cheeks.

"Good. Then my work here is done." He winked at her.

Raz tossed him a sideways smile, shaking her head at his boldness as she stepped away from him.

Seeing the others waiting on the trail up ahead, she whispered. "I need to go. Cassie's waiting."

"I'm right behind you." Luke chuckled behind her. "Oh and Raz? Please don't take any unnecessary risks tonight, okay?"

"I won't." She nodded, grateful for his concern.

She hurried to catch up with her friend, the corners of her lips turned up as she thought about her husband's kisses.

"Couldn't that wait?" One eyebrow raised on Cassie's normally serene face.

Razelle shrugged her shoulders. "Apparently not." She laughed softly, deep inside feeling flattered by Luke's attention.

"Well, now we need to focus." Cassie whispered as they walked softly between the trees. All five of them had talked between themselves about their plan before they crossed the river. They had it worked out — that is, if everything went according to plan.

"Addy's staying in the cabin nearest the wood-burning barrel. But there's a bunch of trees surrounding it, so we should be able to sneak inside." Her friend pointed in the direction of the cabin and Raz nodded following close behind.

As they neared the cabin, Razelle glanced quickly behind them. Luke, Waylon and Hudson were spreading out, ready for any sort of surprise attack.

She breathed easier knowing they were nearby.

Ducking under the tall poplar trees, they crouched against the wall of the cabin.

Cassie put a finger against her lips for the universal signal to remain quiet. Her friend slowly peered around the corner. She waved her hand for Razelle to follow quickly.

Razelle hurried after Cassie through the open door, which she quickly close.

Addy stood in front of them, her hand against her chest as if in shock. "Cassie and Raz… you're here." She burst into tears. "I'm so happy you came back."

"Shh." Razelle hurried to hug Addy. The teenager had become a good friend in the past year that she had come to the camp. "We're here to get you out of here."

"Oh, thank you. Ca… can Olivia come with us too?" At Addy's question, Razelle stepped back and for the first time saw a thin girl sitting on the cot in the corner. Her wide brown eyes and matted hair gave her the look of a frightened mouse.

She looked from Olivia to Cassie and back to Addy. "Of course. We'll bring you both with us."

Addy, sniffed again as fresh tears streamed down her cheeks. "Thanks Razelle."

"We'll need to be really quiet though. We don't want Sloane or his men to find us." Razelle squeezed Addy once more in an embrace before she stepped back.

When she did, Razelle finally got a good look at her eye. "I see you got quite the shiner from Sloane. Can you tell us again what happened?"

Addy nodded. "One day last week, in the middle of the night, Sloane and two of his guards burst into this cabin. I woke up suddenly at the loud crash of the door and so did my friend Cindi — she was here too."

Addy swallowed convulsively, hesitating for a moment before continuing. "Sloane shone the flashlight on me first and then on Cindi. Then he said we'll take that girl for now and the other one can wait until next time."

"He took your friend?" Raz asked softly.

"Yes. Sloane waved for his men to go and then dragged Cindi out of her bed, she was screaming. I ran after Sloane, and tried my hardest to pull his hands off Cindi. That's when he punched me in the eye. I fell to the floor dazed and didn't even get to say goodbye to Cindi." Addy placed both hands over her face, her shoulders shaking with sobs.

Razelle pulled her into a gentle hug, leaning her head against Addy's, sadness and anger at the injustice intermingling at hearing her friend's story.

"You were very brave to defend Cindi." Razelle whispered against her hair.

Addy pulled away shaking her head slightly. "But, I wasn't able to save her. And I don't know where they took her. I'm scared."

Cassie stepped closer. "Did you overhear Sloane or his men say anything about where they were going?"

"I overheard one man say: at least we'll be taking her five states away. Maybe by that time she'll have stopped screaming. Then the other man said: *Well our buyer wanted a fighter and that's what he'll be getting.*" Addy rubbed her hands along her arms as she relayed the incident.

It felt like a lead weight dropped to the pit of Razelle's belly at Addy's words. She looked at Cassie who tried to stifle a gasp.

"Will we be able to find my friend and bring her home?" Addy's fingers tightened on her arm.

Seeing the fear in the teenager's face, Razelle spoke in gentle tones. "We will do everything possible to find Cindi and bring her back home."

Addy expelled the breath she'd been holding and her grip on her arm loosened.

Razelle rubbed her forehead that was aching with worry and fear, doing her best refocus on what they needed to do right now. "This is much worse than we thought. First, we've got to get these girls out of here. We'll deal with the rest later."

Cassie stood frozen for a moment her blue eyes were laced with fear.

Razelle was certain the look in her eyes, matched her own.

"Yes. There's no time to waste." Cassie walked over at

Olivia who still sat hunched over in the corner. "Bundle your stuff up and we can stick them in my backpack."

"We only have a blanket each. That's it." Addy walked to her bed and picked up the blanket.

Razelle took one look at the very dirty blanket and threw it in the corner. "How about we don't worry about it. You'll each have a clean warm blanket waiting for you after we get out of here."

Cassie walked with Olivia to the door. "We have to be extra quiet to get past Sloane and his men."

Addy whispered. "Sloane isn't here right now, I saw him leave this morning. Only his guards are around. They usually roam around the camp at night, each taking turns guarding us. I noticed them a few times, when I needed to use the outhouse."

Razelle walked over to the cracked window near the corner of the cabin and looked outside for guards. "Right now I don't see anyone. I think this might be our chance."

She hurried to the door and opened it a crack. Not seeing anyone near the cabin, she whispered. "Let's go."

Leading the way out the door and down the cabin steps, Razelle grabbed Addy's hand while Cassie held tightly to Olivia's hand.

They had just entered the tree area behind the cabin, when she spotted one of Sloane's guards. Razelle recognized him from all those weeks when she used to come to the camp with Cassie.

The guard must have spotted Luke among the trees, because she saw him step stealthily in Luke's direction.

Razelle tensed. Her only thought was to warn Luke.

She completely forgot about Luke's request not to take

any unnecessary risks. She had never been a passive bystander if someone needed help, and she wouldn't be one now.

Dropping Addy's hand, she rushed forward and yelled. "Luke."

Her voice brought everyone's attention to her.

Luke turned toward her, but he was further away than the guard, who turned and grabbed her, wrapping his arm around her neck.

A surge of panic ran through her body and she struggled to loose herself from his hold.

The guard tightened his grip.

Luke stepped forward, but the guard called out. "Don't move."

He stood still but Luke called out to the three women behind her. "Cassie, take the girls to the boat."

Raz could hear hurried footsteps behind her. She was glad her friends were getting away from this mad man.

Luke challenged the guard. "I think you might find it more of a challenge to fight me."

Another of Sloane's guards called from beside where Razelle was standing. "If you make it worth our while, we might consider it."

"Let go of her and we can fight for the cash in here." Luke pulled out his wallet and opened it so they could see the big wad of greenbacks inside.

"Maybe."

The second guard's eyes widened at the sight of the large handful of cash. "Looks like we hit the jackpot."

At that moment, the first guard loosened his grip

around Raz's neck. The second guard began to walk toward Luke ready to fight him.

She had less than a minute to use the distraction to her advantage. On instinct, she kicked hard at the guard's shin and managed to throw him off balance.

Next, she gave him a shove backwards, and he tumbled to the ground hitting his head on a rock and knocking himself out.

At her quick movement, Luke jumped the second guard, and they were now in a fight.

Luke dodged one punch, but the second one connected with his face. Her husband threw a hard fist, and the guard staggered, but came back swinging.

Razelle looked around for some type of weapon or some way to help. There was nothing she could see.

Finally, Luke shoved the guard up against a tree and with one last punch, knocked him out.

She saw Hudson run up to Luke carrying a rope. After tying both of the guard's hands, Luke grabbed his wallet from the ground and then came back to where she stood.

Luke gave her a quick hug and a worried, searching look. "Are you okay?"

"I'm good." Razelle said, her shaky voice betraying her.

"You're more than good, you are amazing. With those moves you made tonight, I'm lucky to have you on my side."

"I guess I'm just lucky to have learned a few self-defence moves." Razelle's voice shook slightly with every breath.

Luke put his one arm around her shoulders and they hurried toward the river. "Too bad there's no cell phone reception here at the camp, otherwise I'd be calling the police."

Razelle nodded. "We can drive to the police station. They'll want statements from Addy and Olivia anyway."

He nodded. "True. Well let's get going then."

Hudson and Waylon had already gone ahead of them and everyone was waiting in the boat by the time they arrived.

Once they were seated in the boat, Luke spoke. "I might need you to take the oars this time." He waved his swollen hand in Hudson's direction.

"Man, you'll do anything to get out of work won't you?" Chuckling, Hudson grabbed an oar and both Waylon and Hudson paddled the boat to get them across to the other side.

"Oh my gosh, Luke. It looks like your hand is badly sprained or even broken. We need to take you to the Hospital and get a Doctor to take a look at it." Razelle rushed on.

Once they reached the other side, Hud drove them all to the Hospital first.

It didn't take long before Luke came back from seeing the Doctor with his hand wrapped in a tight tensor bandage. "My hand is badly sprained, but not broken."

Razelle expelled a long breath. "Good I'm glad."

She was relieved that all Luke had got was a sprained hand. It could have been much worse.

"Now we can go to the Police station. They can take our statements and then we can finally go home." Luke said, his voice sounded tired and impatient.

Once at the police station, both Addy and Olivia sat

down with the Detective, sharing their experiences at the camp.

After each of them told the police what they had seen and heard, the detective said. "I didn't realize there were so many teenagers at that camp. Your statements will go a long way towards bringing these teenagers out of that camp. We will have some officers look into this right away."

As they walked out of the station, Luke spoke. "I hope they put Sloane's guards in jail. In the morning, I'm going to call a Private Investigator to look into what Sloane is doing and to find that missing girl. Whatever he's doing isn't on the up and up. He needs to be brought to justice."

"I agree." Razelle noticed the dark circles under Luke's eyes. "You're tired. It's time to get home so you can rest that hand."

"I'll be fine. It's a sprain, it'll heal." Luke said pragmatically.

Razelle nodded glad to finally be going back to the cabin.

When they arrived, both Addy and Olivia were yawning and having trouble staying awake. "The girls can sleep in your bedroom?" Luke questioned.

Razelle nodded. Luke had since cleaned out the boxes and put a large bed in her room. Giving the girls her room, was the only practical thing to do under the circumstances. "Of course."

Luke and Razelle helped each of the girls to the room and Razelle stayed to give them towels and show them the washroom.

It wasn't long before both girls were settled under the blankets, and soon were fast asleep.

Luke stood leaning a hip against the kitchen counter, when Razelle came out of their room. "Are they asleep?"

"Yeah. I think all the stress of the day finally caught up with them." Razelle sighed and yawned, placing a hand over her mouth.

"Looks like they aren't the only ones." Luke grinned.

"I know. I'm tired too." Razelle walked to the sink and poured herself a quick glass of water, feeling a little tense.

She wondered what the arrangements going to be for tonight. "Addy and her friend are in my room. Since those girls don't know of our marriage agreement, maybe it's best if I sleep in your room?"

Luke's rogue smile was back. "I can't think of anything I'd like better." Almost as if he could sense her apprehension about their new sleeping arrangements, he whispered. "You go ahead and get settled and I'll join you in awhile."

She nodded, relieved that she would be able to have some privacy. Raz hurried to grab some shorts and a t-shirt from her bedroom.

Walking into Luke's bedroom, she turned on the lamp. The king size bed dominated the room, causing an anxious swirl in her belly.

She started to give herself a stern lecture hoping to regain a better perspective.

You are only sleeping in Luke's bedroom for tonight, so stop being silly. Both of you agreed to a marriage-of-convenience, nothing more. Think of tonight like those days and nights when you and Luke were at Moorea Island. Nothing happened there either. Calm down and stop worrying.

The pep talk she gave herself only helped for a few minutes. As soon as she showered and slipped into her t-shirt and shorts, she was hit by another attack of nerves.

Hurrying to the bed, she shot under the thick blankets and pulled them up to her chin. She desperately wished she could turn off the lamp, but then Luke wouldn't be able to see where he was going.

She tried closing her eyes as if to force her body to sleep, but that didn't work.

The slight creak of the door opening and closing made her aware of Luke's presence.

Thankfully he went straight into the washroom. She rolled onto her side, hoping she would be asleep by the time he crawled into bed.

It was not to be.

Only a few minutes later, she could hear Luke's footsteps on the other side of the large bed. He turned out the lamp and slid under the covers.

Raz was telling herself to go to sleep, when Luke shifted his body and she heard his whisper. "You're not asleep are you?"

It was more of a statement than a question.

There was no use trying to force away the tension any longer. "No. I'm too keyed up to sleep." Razelle rolled over onto her back and her arm bumped into Luke. "Sorry."

"Don't be. I like having you close."

Razelle's heart rate accelerated at his nearness. "I like being close to you too, Luke." She blurted out, realizing too late that maybe she shouldn't have admitted it.

"You really shouldn't tell me that, especially when we're like this." He shifted and his whispered voice sounded closer. All of a sudden he was beside her, his hand reaching out and cupping her chin.

She gasped sharply as Luke's lips touched hers, moving over them slowly, masterfully. A low moan rose deep in her throat, one so soft it was barely audible. It was her small cry of longing and need.

Luke heard it and in answer, eased her closer, wrapping her more fully in his arms. Luke kissed her deeply and hungrily until they were both breathless.

Abruptly, he released her.

"We'd better stop, or soon I won't be able to." Luke pulled away his voice was low and raspy, like he was having difficulty catching his breath.

Raz felt weak and wonderful all at the same time. Despite herself she clung to Luke, her hands gripping his arms.

Luke tasted so warm and familiar, as if she'd spent a lifetime in his arms, as if she were *meant* to spend a lifetime there.

As thoughts of making this a real marriage darted across her mind, she once again wrapped a shield around her heart.

Quickly, she released her grip on his arms and whispered. "You're right we need to stop."

At her side she clenched her hands into fists, trying to control their trembling.

It wasn't fair that with one simple kiss, Luke could make her feel so vulnerable.

She didn't want to feel any of this.

That protective layer around her heart was beginning to crumble, just when she needed to keep it firmly in place.

Beside her Luke released a long sigh, his fingers finding hers, weaving his hand with hers as they lay side by side.

"Why don't we talk instead, since we're both wide awake anyway." She offered to ease the tension between them.

"Sure, what do you want to talk about?" Luke asked as he squeezed her hand.

"Would you tell me the rest of the story of what happened between you and your ex-fiance?" Her voice shook and a shiver ran through her body at the question.

But, even as her body trembled at the thought of learning her husband's deepest secrets, she feared not knowing more.

AT HIS WIFE'S QUESTION, Luke sighed. He knew this talk was coming maybe that's why he'd preferred to be busy.

To be honest, he'd much rather go back to kissing her senseless.

How could he talk about this with Razelle? So far he'd done a good job of avoiding the topic. Somehow he had managed to stay busy, doing his best to push away painful memories and heartache.

She squeezed his hand and Luke embraced the pressure, cradling her smaller hand in his.

Maybe it was time he told her. If he finally told her all

of it, maybe his wife would realize how impossible it was for them to consider any sort of real marriage — or any kind of real future — together.

Razelle whispered in the dark. "What happened? Did you find out why your bride left you at the altar?"

Luke grimaced, thankful their conversation was in the darkness of the room. "Yeah. She left me a note after the wedding that never happened. In the letter, Audra told me she had started dating Nate Caldwell. Nate was an executive in Donovan Oil and made more money and had more prestige."

Luke shook his head. "I should have seen it coming. Audra was constantly asking me what I planned to do after I was done working for Boone. She laughed and mocked me when I told her someday I wanted to run my own cattle ranch. She'd tell me, you'll waste your life by doing that, just like you are wasting your life now being a roustabout."

He paused remembering. "I guess she finally found someone who gave her what she wanted — more money and prestige than I had at the time."

"It was her mistake that she didn't see who the real you."

"To be honest, I don't think I saw who she really was either, or the issues she was dealing with. At some point during our dating life, I learned she was bi-polar and had to take daily medication. It made sense when I learned what happened next."

"What happened?"

"After Audra left me at the altar, I wasn't surprised to

hear about her dating Nate Caldwell." Luke swallowed the dark memories.

"The real shock came just a couple weeks later. I learned from a friend that Nate and Audra broke up and the next day my ex-fiance ended up overdosing on prescription meds and died."

Luke ran a hand through his hair as new waves of guilt washed over him.

"That's horrible. I'm so sorry, Luke." Raz's eyes glistened with moisture and a few tears trailed down her cheeks. "I'm sorry to hear about your ex-fiance. Sounds like there were many difficult things she was dealing with." Razelle shifted and placed a hand on his cheek.

She wiped away tears he didn't realize had drifted down his cheek.

Luke's shoulders shook as sobs ripped through him.

She leaned her head on his shoulder and wrapped her arm around him. "Let all the pain out, Luke. You need to grieve. You must have loved your ex-fiance very much."

Suddenly he turned, venting his anger and grief. "No, I didn't love Audra as much as I should have. If I had, somehow I would have known the depths of her pain. I would have made sure I continued to talk to her and I'd have done something to stop her from dying."

He barely caught his breath before continuing. "I didn't love her like I should have. My selfish neglect of her is the reason she died. I'm the reason Audra killed herself."

"No, that's not true Luke. She broke up with you and moved on." Razelle tried to reason with him.

"She might have ended it between us, but it might have been exactly what set the downward spiral in motion for

Audra." Luke shook his head as all the pain in his heart exploded to the surface at once.

"I've been selfish and uncaring for so long, that's why it's finally coming back around like I deserve." He truly believed his words.

"Luke that's not true…" He interrupted her. Razelle didn't understand.

"It is true." The way Luke saw it, everything was coming full circle and he was finally getting what he deserved. "I should have been a better son and maybe that would've helped lessen the stress my Dad went through with his business partner's betrayal. Because of that neglect on my part, it cost my Dad his life."

Luke expelled a sharp breath. "I brought shame on my mom, brothers and grandparents because after Dad died, I lost who I was for awhile and hung out with the wrong crowd — the partying, drinking and drug crowd. I failed my family and I failed my ex-fiance."

As wave after wave of painful memories washed over Luke, he couldn't lie there any longer. He moved so that he sat up in the bed, leaning his head against the headboard.

Razelle shifted until she sat beside him. She leaned close, leaning her head against his shoulder almost as if being physically close to him, she could take away his pain.

"Tonight, when that guard grabbed you, I thought I'd lost you and my heart nearly stopped." A shudder ran through his body as he thought about it. "It was like losing my dad and my ex-fiance all over again. I didn't protect you like I should have."

He released a labored breath. "Looking back, I finally see clearly. If I'd been a better man — less selfish and neglectful of those I cared about — I wouldn't have caused so much pain to the people I love. And just maybe, Audra wouldn't have killed herself."

Luke could feel Raz's shoulders shaking and heard her gentle sobs as she sat beside him. Wrapping his arm around her shoulders, he pulled her close, kissing the top of her head.

"I'm so sorry, Luke." She grabbed his hand that hung down her shoulder. "I'm sorry for every loss. I'm sorry for all your heartache. I'm sorry for all the pain you went through. But, you don't need to be alone any longer. We can get through this together."

Luke sat there frozen in the stillness of the night. And his body tensed as memories coursed through him of how he'd failed those he loved.

He'd failed himself and didn't deserve his wife's continued understanding, compassion and acceptance.

Didn't she understand?

His voice came out fiercer than before. "Now that you've got a good look at the selfish man that I've become Razelle, I'm sure you can see why I've closed myself off to most of the world. Do you really think anyone, any woman, would truly want to be in a real marriage to a man like me?"

Her body flinched at his harsh judgement of who he was.

Luke believed in total honesty between them.

Far better that he learn that Razelle hated him than to repeat the same mistake he made with his ex-fiance.

Then why did fear coil in his belly, like a loaded spring as if waiting for her to reject him?

※

SHOCK FLUTTERED THROUGH RAZELLE.

She couldn't move for a moment as she absorbed her husband's harsh words. She hadn't realized how much anger he held inside from all he'd gone through.

His anger and unforgiveness of himself had spread like a poison through his whole body.

As her husband shared his story of pain and heartache, tears streamed down her cheeks. Razelle sat beside him frozen to the spot as a new awareness dawned.

Her husband was terrified of getting close to another woman. The thought of going through deep pain was what held him back from loving again.

He was afraid he would not measure up, that he could never truly be loved again because of all the mistakes in his past.

"Luke," She breathed his name and reached up, her fingertips gently cupping his cheek. He trembled under her touch but didn't move away.

She leaned closer, pulling his head down to her even as she stretched to meet him. Razelle pressed her lips gently to his forehead, his eyelids, his cheeks and finally to his lips.

Luke tightened his hands on her shoulders and she felt his body shudder against her. "Raz… don't."

She continued kissing him.

"All the pain, heartache and fears are part of who you are." She whispered.

"As I've come to know you, the real Luke Stevenson, all I see is the kind, generous and loving man that you are." She was so close, their breath mingled as one. "And any woman would want to be married to an amazing man like you."

Luke was silent and his fingertips toyed with her hair and he pulled her close.

"I don't deserve you, Razelle. You are far too good for a man like me. There's too much pain and hurt inside me that if you get too close, I'm worried it'll spread like a virus and infect you too." Luke kissed the top of her head, sighing heavily.

"No you won't infect me Luke. You just need a chance to heal…" Razelle began but Luke interrupted her.

"I can't do this to you. I can't dump all my failures onto you. I can't cause you that kind of pain." Luke stiffened beside her and his whispered words were hurried. "Raz, don't think of me. Don't dream of me. Don't fall in love with me. I'm no good for you or for any woman."

Razelle wanted to stop the rant of negative words, but he went on. "We'll stick to our original agreement. Then, after a year, you'll be free to find a man who isn't broken and filled with poison. Someone, who is much better than me."

Luke kissed the top of her head. The broken sigh that rippled through his body, shook hers to the core.

"Good night." He slid down under the covers and turned his back to her.

Razelle sat there for a moment, unmoving.

What had just happened?

One moment her husband was sharing the deepest parts of his heart and in the next moment he shut himself off from her. *It seemed almost as if he was shutting down any closeness between them.*

Luke was letting fear come between them.

Her husband was desperate to get away from what he saw as his own failures, mistakes and heartache.

She knew he needed to forgive himself so he could be free to love again.

Would her love for her husband be enough to help him heal?

uke

LUKE DROVE his truck down the dirt road that led to one of Donovan's properties and the camping site on the southernmost tip of Paradise Lake.

Hitched to the truck was a long Camper trailer, perfect for weekend trips to the lake.

He was happy they were going to spend some time at the lake with the Donovan family. It was difficult for their family, especially this time of year.

Shifting in the seat beside him, his wife turned her eyes full of questions. "Tell me again why the Donovan family invited us on this weekend camping trip?"

Luke nodded. "Every year around this time, Millie and Boone and their now adult children, go spend time at the lake. They remember their daughter, Waylon's twin sister, who died years ago. Ever since I became friends with Waylon and Hudson in Middle School, they've asked me to join them."

Usually, this was a camping trip that he did out of loyalty and duty, but this year he was eager to go. If nothing else, he hoped this time away would be a distraction and help ease the tension between his wife and himself.

Since their serious heart to heart chat two nights ago, they had both been tiptoeing around each other. He hadn't meant to hurt his wife, but he'd needed to tell her the truth as he saw it.

He hoped this camping trip would put a smile on Razelle's face. Luke wanted to see her happy, even if he couldn't be the one to give it to her.

"That's so sad that their daughter died years ago. I don't remember Millie mentioning it at dinner last night." She pulled her long braid over her shoulder and twisted her fingers through the thick auburn weave.

He thought back to last night's dinner and the sad mood that always accompanied their annual dinners and camping trip.

This time was a little different. For Luke, it made things a little more cheery that Razelle was included in the invitation.

He explained. "Neither Boone or Millie like to dwell on the details of their daughter's death. Instead, they focus on remembering the wonderful things about her every year and do their best to help Waylon do the same."

"Does Waylon feel extra miserable because of his twin

sister's death?" A deep sadness filled Razelle as she thought of what Waylon was going through.

She could imagine that it would be extra difficult to lose your twin. In fact, there were a few times when she had dreams as a little girl about having a sibling the same age with whom she had a deep bond.

But, when she'd wake up in the morning Raz couldn't help but be a little sad as she remembered that it was only her and her Mother.

"Yeah." Luke nodded. "Every year around this time, Waylon gets quite depressed."

Razelle felt bad for him. "Well, maybe we can all cheer him up."

"That's Millie's plan. We'll do what we can." They arrived at Donovan's lakeside property. Luke backed the Camper near some trees for shade.

Luke's phone rang a few times before he answered. "It's good to hear from you Steve. Any news?"

Steve's monotone voice spoke on the other end of the line. "I just learned that Cindi, the girl that disappeared from the camp, is being held in a house with other teenagers in downtown Detroit. There are three pimps that run the place and it looks like they are under lock and key."

Steve Massey, his Private Investigator, gave him a little more information on the place.

"Do you have an address?" Luke asked, quickly writing it down. "Thanks Steve. Can you meet me tomorrow morning at the Police Station? Yes, they'll take our statement."

Luke hung up the phone, looking over at Razelle. "They found Cindi."

"Oh, thank God." Her mouth fell open and she closed it quickly at the news. "The police will get her out of there?"

"Yes. And we'll need to tell them what we know about Sloane and his men, but they'll be going to jail." Luke couldn't help but feel happy that justice was finally going to be done and these teenagers would be free from their human trafficking predators.

"Luke, I'm so glad. Will they bring Cindi to the Stevenson Safe House to be with Addy and Olivia?"

"Yes. I'll double check what the plan is, when I go to the police station tomorrow." Luke saw his wife's green eyes filled with moisture. "Happy?"

"Yes. I'm happy that finally those teenagers can truly begin healing and get back to normal life." Razelle felt her heart squeezing in grief at the thought of what those girls must be going through.

They both stepped out of the truck and within minutes Millie was there to greet them. "Oh, I'm so glad you two are here. And Razelle, I'm especially happy you've joined us. I need another woman to chat with, when I'm surrounded by all these men."

Mrs. Donovan winked at Luke who laughed and said. "Millie, you've had no difficulty handling yourself despite being surrounded by the men in your life."

Mrs. Donovan laughed out loud. "You're right of course. But I would still like to spend time with Razelle, woman to woman. When you're ready Luke, come join us by the fire. Boone and my three sons are setting things up so we can have a nice picnic and campfire by the lake."

"I'll be there soon." Luke waved, and chuckled as he unlocked the camper's hitch from the truck.

Standing up once again, he watched as Millie slipped her arm around Razelle and they walked together down toward the lake.

He grinned, happy his wife had a mom figure in her life like in Millie Donovan.

She was a kind woman who would give Razelle the love of a mother that she had been missing for most of her life.

Luke hurried toward the lake eager to enjoy time with his wife and the Donovan family.

MILLIE'S ARM hung lightly on Razelle's waist as they walked toward the lake.

The sun was beginning to lower, weaving a path across the blue water. The sun's rays pointed in the direction of the campfire, which seemed like a gentle nod in their direction.

"I love sitting by a campfire by the lake. When you add the orange red colors of a sunset, it's so beautiful." Millie's green eyes stared out at where the sun met the water for a long moment.

When she turned, Razelle saw tears fill Millie's eyes.

"So many memories. That's what tonight is about. I'm glad you and Luke could join us." Millie squeezed her shoulder. They reached the beach and Millie went straight to her husband and was enveloped in a gentle hug.

Razelle thought she'd never seen anything more beautiful. What a great love they must have had all these years to withstand the turbulent storms they had obviously gone through as a family.

"Hey, Razelle. Want me to whittle you a stick for Smores?" Waylon stood near the roaring campfire, holding a whittling knife in one hand.

"Sure, Waylon. Do you want help?"

"Come on." Waylon gestured for her to follow him. She hurried to catch up with him. When they reached the line of trees they looked around trying to find branches that were sturdy but not too thick.

Waylon looked up and pointed. "There's one. Do you want to grab that tree branch, Razelle? I'll help you reach it." As soon as those words left his mouth, she had a quick impression of a little boy her age asking her the same question. Except, she remembered he called her Rosa. *Rosa, grab that tree branch. It's just the right size. I'll help you reach up.*

Closing her eyes, she shook her head, trying to shake off the strange image that formed in her head.

"You okay?" Waylon interrupted her thoughts. "You look a little pale."

Swallowing, she nodded. "I'm good, thanks. But if you don't mind, I'm going to get back to the campfire and sit down for a minute."

"Sure." Waylon watched her for a minute before he went back to search for more branches.

With her limbs shaking, Razelle walked back to what now was a blazing campfire and sat down on the large log-bench.

The mental image she experienced when she'd been

with Waylon, scared her. At first she thought it was a memory from when she was a little child, but she shoved down that thought and assumed she was more tired than she realized.

Before long, Luke joined her on the log-bench and Hudson, Waylon and Sawyer soon after.

Razelle looked over a Waylon whose green eyes held a haunted look.

Boone began talking. "It's good to be here again as a family… and yes Luke and Razelle we include you both in that." Boone winked at them. "All of us are here tonight to remember little Rosalyn, our little girl who died when she was only three years old."

Boone paused and swallowed a surge of emotions. "Thought it might be nice if each of us could share what we remember about her. I'll begin. I remember her loud belly laugh whenever I would throw her in the air. She would yell out, 'catch me daddy!' She trusted me to not let her go." A crack sounded in Boone's voice and he hesitated for a moment.

"I loved to play that game with her… a treasured memory I'll never forget. So, if anyone else has a special memory to share, we'd love to hear it."

Razelle sucked in a breath as memories came back to her of dreams she used to have when she was four and five. She would dream of being thrown in the air by her daddy and he would catch her. In her dreams, they would play it over and over again.

She tried to shake off the memories. This wasn't about her, this was about the Donovan family remembering the little girl they lost years ago.

Hudson began. "I remember Rosalyn loved to play with the kittens on the farm when we lived in Texas. I remember the one day she had five of them on her little lap petting each one in turn. They were happy as clams."

Millie grinned, her eyes a little misty.

Sawyer spoke softly. "My little sister used to follow me to the barn. She'd always point to the horse and say 'ride.' So we'd get on the horse. She'd sit on the front of the saddle and I'd take her for around the pasture. I always loved to see her big smile."

"I remember you doing that. I could tell when I heard her giggling, that she loved that." Boone shook his head and chuckled at the memory.

"Waylon, how about you?" Boone looked at his youngest son, his voice gentle.

Razelle glanced his way, feeling a tug on her heart as her gaze met his eyes — haunted and shrunken. It was almost as if she could feel his deep sorrow and regret.

Without thinking she grabbed Luke's hand and squeezed, some part of her needing a lifeline to hang onto.

Luke shifted to sit a little closer and he held her hand in both of his.

Waylon expelled a heavy sigh and whispered. "As her twin, I remember feeling so close to Rosa that it was like we could hear each other's thoughts. Her green eyes would light up with delight at the idea of going to the lake. Which is exactly what happened that tragic day eighteen years ago."

Waylon's voice cracked with emotion and he swallowed convulsively before continuing. "We had just got to our camping spot at the lake and mom and dad were bringing the food to the camp table and dad was chopping wood for a fire."

He hesitated before going on. "Sawyer and Hudson were off chasing our dog or something. So I grabbed Rosa's hand and we went to the water. We were at a spot by the lake, sort of hidden by some bushes. Anyway, like usual, we started looking for water creatures under the water. We were only three years old, so I don't know what we expected to find."

He chuckled softly. "We were busy digging under the water, when suddenly I heard what sounded like mom's voice calling my name. 'Waylon come here. I need your help.' I told Rosa I'd be right back and she didn't say anything but continued digging in the water."

"I ran to Mom and asked her why she called my name. Mom told me she didn't call for me." Waylon looked over at Millie who nodded. "Then she asked where Rosa was and I told her. Mom hurried to where we had been playing on the edge of the lake, only Rosa wasn't there.

Waylon's voice choked up. "We looked and looked for her, not finding her. Later on, when the police dug through the water around the area where we'd been playing, they found her water shoes and the hat she'd been wearing. It was stuck under a rock not far from where we'd been playing."

Tears streamed down Waylon's cheeks as memories of that day came back. "If only I hadn't grabbed Rosa's hand to pull her to the water in the first place. Then later, if I hadn't left her there by herself, she wouldn't have died. It's my fault she's gone."

Waylon's shoulders shook as he sobbed with the loss of

his sister. Millie hurried over and going down on her knees pulled her son into a tight embrace. "No son. It's not your fault. You were only a child, you didn't know."

As Waylon shared the story of how they lost his twin sister, Razelle felt as if she could picture what happened that day in her mind so great was her empathy towards him. Her own tears flowed down her cheeks and she wiped her wet face with her sleeves. Luke shifted closer and placed his arm around her shoulders.

Seeing Millie hold her youngest son, rocking him back and forth, caused Razelle's tears to flow harder. Something about the tender bond they shared as Mother and child, made her realize that she'd missed so many tender moments. She'd missed having a deep bond with a Mother that loved her.

Millie's gentle voice could be heard even in the middle of the tears. "Let's bring the flowers, Waylon. You can set it to float this year, son. Okay?"

Mrs. Donovan reached for her son's hand and he clasped hers. Waylon followed his mother, holding her hand tightly.

Millie found the flowers. "You can join us, if you like. We're going to give Rosalyn the flowers she loves and give her a proper send off."

Razelle held Luke's hand and they walked together behind the rest of the Donovan family.

She couldn't shake the feeling all evening, that so much what she was seeing and hearing was familiar. But that didn't make any sense to her.

Millie held up the flowers in her hand so everyone could see. "We put Rosa's favorite flowers, roses, lilies, peonies and orchids, into the shape of a crown. I always remember how she followed me into the garden, especially loving the herbs and flowers."

Millie's lips quivered as she spoke. "I would hold her in my arms, and she would lean over, reach for a few flowers and say in her cute three year old voice: *Mama smells like the garden. I want to too.* Then she would rub the flowers all over her face and clothes." Millie laughed softly at the memory.

She handed Waylon the flowers shaped in a crown. "Often we would sing our favourite made-up song. It went a little like this: *Rosa, Rosa, little me; how I wonder who you'll be; up above you reach for the stars; You're a diamond — that's who you are; Rosa Rosa little me, how I wonder who you'll be.*"

Waylon joined in the song singing with Millie.

Without thinking, Razelle started singing along, knowing the song from memory.

Suddenly, Millie turned as she heard Razelle's voice joining them.

Millie Donovan walked over to Razelle, standing in front of her reaching out to grab her hands. "How do you know the words to that song?"

Razelle stood there staring at Millie, shocked. It was like a whole bunch of memories suddenly returned.

She remembered her Dad lifting her high in the air.

She remembered riding the horse with Sawyer.

She remembered being in the garden with her Mother.

And she remembered that day by the water, with her twin brother Waylon.

"I remember it all now. It's coming back to me." Tears

streamed down Razelle's cheeks. She glanced at Luke and back at Millie Donovan. "I know the song, because I remember you singing it to me when I was little."

Millie's chin quivered, shock registering on her face. Slowly, she raised her hands to gently touch Razelle's cheeks. "You're my Rosalyn? How can that be? She died years ago."

"Yeah. They didn't find little Rosa. The police even searched through the missing persons database, and couldn't find her." Sawyer spoke out, his brows furrowed with uncertainty. "So, how do we know for sure you are really Rosa?"

Waylon walked up to her. "There's one way to know for sure. We're twins. Let me see if you still have the birthmark on your right shoulder that's in the shape of half a heart."

Razelle nodded. "Of course." She rolled up the sleeve of her t-shirt and showed the Donovan family her arm.

"I can't believe it." Millie breathed, both hands covering her lips. "You're Rosalyn. My daughter is truly alive."

Millie Donovan embraced her like she'd never let her go again. Soon all the Donovan's were hugging her, with tears streaming down their cheeks.

"Our Rosalyn is back with us." Millie breathed again and again, holding Razelle's hand.

"It might take me a little time getting used to being called Rosalyn again, Millie." Raz whispered.

Millie stopped her. "That's okay. It won't take you long. And I'd be pleased if you called me Mom." Her voice faltered. "I finally have my little girl back, and I want to hear those precious words from your lips."

Razelle drew her Mom into a close embrace, still in shock that Millie and Boone Donovan were her real parents.

She had so many questions.

How did she end up living with Angelique Chattaine, the person who said she was her Mother for the last eighteen years?

Razelle was desperate for answers.

"WAIT JUST A SECOND. WE NEED ANSWERS." Boone Donovan led the way and they all sat back down by the campfire.

Boone rubbed a hand through his hair as he thought things through. "If you didn't actually die that day when you were three years old, what happened to you? And who exactly is the person that raised you?"

Razelle was grateful for Luke's arm around her shoulders.

At this moment her husband was like the tower of strength she needed to make it through the difficult questions that were about to come her way.

"As for the first question, I remember a little something about that day by the lake." Razelle looked at Waylon who grinned.

"Share what you remember, Rosa. It's probably a little different than my memory of the day." Waylon nodded for her to go on.

Raz startled a little at the being called Rosa, but she didn't mind. It made her feel closer to her family. "Okay. Well, it happened like Waylon said, except when he thought he heard Mom's voice calling, I saw this woman with black hair standing behind my brother."

Her voice shook. "When he hurried off to find our Mom, the woman quickly grabbed me and took off my shoes and my hat. She ran into the water and left my hat and shoes there. She gave me candy to suck on and carried me on her hip."

"Maybe it was because I had candy in my mouth that I didn't call out? I don't know. But that's what I remember." Razelle shuddered to think that the Mother that raised her from three years of age had actually stolen her from her real parents.

Boone's voice was low, coming out like a growl. "Do you have a picture of this woman?"

"Yeah, who is she?" Hudson's tone filled with protective anger.

Razelle reached into her pocket and pulled out her smartphone.

Seeing the picture of Angelique Chattaine, the woman whom she'd called Mother all these years, made her angry. How could she have done this to her?

Razelle passed her smartphone to Boone Donovan — her father.

"This woman is the person who raised you?" Boone's voice boomed out in anger and he clenched his hand into a fist. "Millie, you are not going to believe this." He showed the picture to his wife.

"Maggie Dillan." Millie gasped as she looked at the photo.

"How do you know her?" Razelle rubbed her arms as a sudden chill took over her body.

Boone stood to his feet and began pacing. "We grew up with Maggie. She was our friend."

"And your fiance for a short time…" Millie interrupted, her gaze meeting her husband's.

"Yes, although that was a poor choice on my part." Boone conceded.

Millie nodded and smiled. "I agree."

"But, Maggie disappeared from our small town in Texas, right after her grandparents died. Do you remember Millie?" Boone paced as he searched for answers.

"I do remember. And it was also around that same time that our little girl went missing." Millie wiped a stray tear from her cheek. She looked up at her husband with a strange expression on her face. "You don't think Maggie would have taken our little girl, to exact some sort of revenge on us?"

"I don't know. Maybe we'll never know. But we do need to let the police know." Boone stated firmly.

Luke nodded. "That's probably the best course of action. Maggie as you call her, goes by the name Angelique Chattaine."

Luke explained. "She has a coffee shop called Angelique's cafe, where her and Razelle lived and worked. I could tell by our chat, that she definitely feels like she's losing control and doing whatever she can to fight back."

Luke described the confrontation he'd had with Angelique at his office building.

Waylon huffed. "Angelique Chatelaine. Well I certainly understand why she felt the need to change her name, since she stole my sister." His voice was low and filled with anger.

It warmed her to hear her brother and father defending her and treating her like family. It felt so surreal, that she was now part of this family.

"Maggie always was prideful and stubborn. What I'd really like to do is go down to her coffee shop and give her a piece of my mind." Boone was ranting, getting it out of his system.

"Boone, dear. I think it's better if we tell the police what's happened and let them handle it." Millie stood to her feet and walked over to her husband, grabbing his hands and her gaze meeting his.

"I know you're right, Millie. I just get so angry when I think of what Maggie's done." A vein popped in Boone's neck and his voice shook.

Millie rubbed a hand along his cheek. "I understand. I'm angry too. But this time, instead of going all maverick and handling on your own, let's talk to the police."

Razelle was grateful her birth Mom could talk her Dad off the emotional cliff he was on, before he did something he'd regret.

"All right, you win." Boone expelled a heavy sigh. "Well, there's no time to waste then. Let's go to the police."

"Then we can finally live a normal life and our family will be together and safe from that horrible woman." Boone grabbed his wife's hand and she smiled.

Soon, Razelle and Luke were following the Donovan family as they drove toward the police station. She had never expected today would end like this.

It was a day filled with surprising revelations, both bad and good.

Even as she gave a prayer of thanks for her newfound family, Razelle worried that it might not be an easy road to bring Angelique Chattaine to justice.

She knew her Mother -- her fake Mother well.

She hoped the police would act quickly, because if they didn't Angelique might disappear again with no trace.

Razelle breathed a sigh of relief that soon she would be safe from the woman who had caused such heartache in her life.

CHAPTER FIFTEEN

azelle

Tossing and turning, Razelle woke up as the morning sun poked through a crack in her curtains and landed on her nose.

As she squinted into the sunlight, she thought of Luke. A warm glow of happiness flooded through her.

Last night she dreamed that her and Luke had two children and that her real parents, Boone and Millie Donovan were a big part of their lives.

With a big smile on her face she quietly got dressed, slipping on jeans and t-shirt.

Quietly, so as not to wake up Luke, she walked to the kitchen.

Her cat Sunbeam was letting her know it was time for food.

Raz opened a can of cat food and quickly placed it into her bowl.

She made coffee and poured the hot drink into her favorite mug. Glancing out the window, she noticed the weather was calm. It was a perfect day for a walk to the bridge.

Razelle wrote a hurried note. *Went for a walk to my favorite thinking place. I'll be back to have breakfast with you. Yours Razelle.*

As she walked, soothing sounds came from all around her. The birds chirping in the trees and the sounds of cattle and horses from the farms near the path, made her think of happy summer days.

Reaching her favorite spot on the walking bridge, she sat down swinging her legs over the wooden ledge. Picking up her mug of coffee she savored each sip, her thoughts on all that had happened yesterday.

First, she regained her memories and discovered that Boone and Millie were her real parents. She smiled and warmth filled her at the thought that she now had three brothers and two loving parents as her real family.

She was still in shock, but very grateful.

When the police took their statements about what they knew of Maggie Dillan, she'd found it difficult to talk about her childhood with her Mother.

But, she'd shared everything she remembered with the two detectives.

Now that was over, thank God. She hoped she would never need to see Maggie Dillan again.

The rippling of the water below soothed her anxious thoughts.

Soon, she began dreaming of having a real life with Luke.

Razelle could admit that she really, truly loved him. He'd helped her through so many difficult times and was always there for her, ready with encouragement or advice.

She was ready to give him her heart, but Luke still held himself back from her. He didn't think he was good enough to be her real husband. How could she make Luke see that they would be so good together?

Razelle's gaze was drawn to the river below, hoping to find the answers she was seeking.

Without warning a voice called her name. "Razelle, here you are. I knew it wouldn't be hard to find you. You are so predictable."

Her Mother's low cool tones sent a warning shot through her that she remembered all too well. This tone of voice — a syrupy sweet tone — meant she was very angry.

A chill slid over her.

As if in a trance Razelle slowly turned her head and saw her Mother.

With a calculated look, Maggie Dillan quickly pulled out a gun, pointing it straight at her heart.

FOR THE THIRD time that morning, Razelle tried to pull her hands free of the handcuffs.

Why had she decided to go for a walk to the bridge. She scolded herself. *Razelle, that was stupid. Why didn't you remember Mother knew you took regular walks there?*

But, no matter how much she chastised herself, it didn't change what happened. The fact was, Maggie now held her in handcuffs and at gunpoint until they reached their destination.

This was their fourth day driving and they were now in Texas. Each day they had switched to a different vehicle.

She was convinced Maggie was trying to stop the police from learning their whereabouts.

Razelle still didn't know where Maggie was taking her and the unknown worried her.

"You won't be able to get free of them. So just relax and enjoy the ride." Her Mother lowered the window of her car and puffed on her cigarette, blowing out rings of smoke as she spoke.

"You know that detective you spoke to a few days ago is a particular friend of mine. He's the one who called to warn me what you and your real family were up to."

Maggie went on. "How you could make a statement to the police against your own Mother, is beyond me. Don't you have any loyalty?" This woman who Razelle now knew as Maggie Dillan, continued ranting.

How could Maggie expect loyalty, when she had been the one to steal her from her real mom?

"You're not my real Mother. Millie Donovan is my real..." Razelle began to explain, but was cut off.

"Quiet!" Maggie hissed. "I don't want to even hear that woman's name."

She should have known talking about Millie Donovan, would be a sore point with Maggie.

Maggie.

That's how she would think of the woman who pretended to be her real Mother for all these years.

Razelle was angry with her for all the mental torment Maggie had brought on her and her real family all these years.

"You know what your precious Millie Donovan did to me?" Maggie continued with cool detached tones, as if her outburst hadn't happened at all.

"We were friends in high school. Did she tell you that? No of course she didn't. But we were. In fact, we were best friends for all of High School, until I started dating Boone Donovan."

Razelle wasn't sure she wanted to hear this story from Maggie certain she would find a way to twist the truth.

"Yes, I really liked Boone Donovan. In fact, after High School we continued to date until one day he asked me to marry him. We were engaged. It only lasted for a couple of months, however."

"I went away to nursing school and by the time I got back, Boone wanted to call off the engagement. He said he didn't love me anymore. I gave him back the ring, certain I could bring him around again, given time." Maggie took an extra long drag from her cigarette, brows furrowed in anger.

"But that wasn't to be. One day I saw Boone at his parents' farm, he was kissing my best friend Millie. Only two short months later, they were married. I've never felt so betrayed in my life."

They had reached an old farmyard out in the dry prairies. It was an out of the way place, as Razelle hadn't seen anyone for miles.

Maggie stopped the car and got out opening her door.

"We've finally made it." Maggie paused and looked around. "This ugly farmhouse is what my loving grandparents gave me." Maggie's voice dripped with sarcasm.

"It's a nice farm. Maybe they meant well."

"No, Gramps did not mean well." Maggie opened the door and Razelle walked inside knots of fear in her belly. There were cobwebs everywhere, giving the place a feeling like that of a haunted house. "Let's go downstairs."

She opened a door, and Razelle saw old stairs leading to the cave-like depth below.

Maggie pointed the gun she held in her hand at her. "You go first."

Razelle limbs shook with each step, certain Maggie was leading her down there to rot. Reaching the bottom, she walked to the middle of the large empty space, looking around.

Only one tiny window was seen at the top of the cement wall. The rest of the basement lay hidden in darkness.

"Gramps was so proud that he built his house with a large cement basement. He sure used it enough, locking me down here when I did something he didn't agree with." Maggie sighed.

"That was part of the reason I was in a hurry to marry Boone Donovan. I was desperate to get away from Gramps. But, like anyone I've ever trusted, Boone and Millie betrayed me."

"I'm sure they didn't mean to betray you, they just fell in love." Razelle tried to get Maggie to see reason, but she wasn't having any of it.

Maggie's voice was oddly chilling. "Boone Donovan loved me. He was mine. Millie took him from me. I don't take kindly to anyone taking stuff from me — or for that matter when someone leaves me."

Her cold, pointed look at Razelle caused her arms and legs to tremble. "They betrayed me, pure and simple. Just like you did."

Raz had left the person she believed to be her Mother, because Maggie had become so controlling she hadn't been able to stand it anymore.

Looking at Maggie now, it seemed nothing had changed. If anything, she had gotten worse.

As she thought of all the years Maggie had controlled her, all of a sudden she remembered her talk with Mamie.

Bravely Razelle spoke, reminding herself that at this point she didn't have much to lose. "Speaking of betrayal, Grandmere told me she never got the letters I wrote when we moved to Washington State. Did you mail them?"

Raz stared at Maggie as she waited for an answer.

Maggie's dark eyes narrowed and shot daggers at Raz before she spoke. "I did not mail those letters, I threw them in the trash where they belonged."

Shaking her head, Maggie continued with her tirade. "Did you honestly think I would allow you to write to your Mamie and continue your close relationship with her? You were supposed to be *my daughter* and be close to me, not to that old woman."

"But, she was so good to me. I grew to love her." Raz whispered, tears pricking at the back of her eyes.

"Well, that's your problem. You should be more careful

who you let yourself love. Trust me, almost every time they will let you down. I hope that taught you a lesson."

Razelle sucked in a breath, suddenly finding it hard to breathe. How could the woman who had raised her, be so cruel?

"Now, no more questions. I've heard enough." Maggie commanded and pointed to the only chair in the large cavernous room. "Sit down."

Razelle slowly sat down, curling her legs tightly under the chair. Her hands were stiff in the handcuffs, but more than that her belly coiled in fear, wondering what Maggie had planned.

Maggie quickly reached for a rope and tied her legs tightly together. The rope bit into her skin and her legs ached.

The woman who used to be her mother, walked into a different room and came back a moment later carrying a chair in one hand and a clock in the other hand. There were a bunch of wires attached to the clock, which looked strange.

As Maggie adjusted the clock she spoke. "I always thought you would be with me until my old age Razelle. When I took you from Millie and Donovan that day at the lake, I was sure I was doing you a favor."

Her voice wounded childlike and shrunken. "I told myself at last you would be with a Mother who would take you away from parents who couldn't be trusted. But now, I realize that you can't be trusted either. You aren't loyal. You betrayed me too. It must be in your blood."

"Gramps used to tell me, you can always tell problems with people because it shows in their bloodline." She faced

Razelle, her gaze pointed. "Maybe that's the one thing he got right."

"I am trustworthy. The problem was you tried to control me, a twenty-one year old adult. I didn't want to live like that anymore." Razelle tried to reason with her.

Maggie gave a brittle laugh. "See what I mean? You didn't want to live like that. What about what I wanted?"

She paused and turned to set something on the clock. "But to prove I've forgiven you, I've decided today to give you extra time. Do you see this clock? It's a countdown timer. When it reaches zero, it will blow the roof off this house — and sadly, you'll go with it."

"But I've set the timer to one hour instead of five minutes, which should give you enough time to reflect on everything you've done wrong and ask for forgiveness."

Something heavy landed in the bottom of Raz's stomach. Like a ball of fear, it doubled in weight, settling lower and heavier. Pulling everything inside her along with it.

There was something cold and snake-like that weaved its way up from the pit of Razelle's stomach, leaving a trail of ice in its wake. It felt much like a Roto-Rooter worming through her veins, sucking up all her blood.

"What do you mean?" Raz called out as Maggie walked toward the stairs.

Maggie didn't answer and instead waved. "See you much, much later, daughter." Maggie's syrupy sweet voice called out as she walked up the stairs.

Razelle, sat there alone and fear flooded her body.

Was this the end? Was she literally about to die?

Staring at the countdown timer, she noticed it had

already reached forty-five minutes. This couldn't be happening to her.

She told herself to calm down and begin thinking. She was unsure if there was anything she could do to get out of this mess.

Looking down at the handcuffs on her hands and seeing her feet tied together with a tight rope, it seemed she was stuck.

She said a quick prayer for help.

Memories of all the years of her Mother confining her to tight places began a fear of small spaces from childhood.

Right now that fear was growing and threatened to overpower rational thought.

Mentally Raz pushed away the terror that filled every cell of her being. A sharp pain gnawed between her eyes at her predicament.

Her hands and feet grew cold and stiff and she moved them as much as she could.

Looking down at the handcuffs, she saw the place where Maggie had stuck the key in to lock them. She'd done that each day on their road trip.

Razelle suddenly remembered she was wearing her necklace key from Mamie.

Mamie's words came back when she'd first given her the key to the music box: *You are growing from a caterpillar and stretching into a beautiful butterfly. Someday you will have the freedom to spread your wings and fly.*

She had do this.

If she could somehow get the key off her neck, maybe

she could stick it inside the hole of the handcuffs to open them.

It was worth a try.

Lifting her cuffed hands, she pushed the gold chain up past her chin, but it fell back down. After five tries, the chain finally made it over her head, landing on top of her handcuffs.

She couldn't use her hands, so how was she going to grab the key?

Suddenly she remembered a few times she had to put a pin in her mouth to open the lock in a door back at home.

Razelle decided it was worth a try.

Lifting up her handcuffed hands, she leaned over and after a few tries, was finally able to put the key in her mouth.

Twisting it in her mouth until it was finally facing the right direction, Razelle once again lifted the handcuffs so the keyhole faced her.

It took real focus, but finally she positioned the key in the hole. She was grateful that the key from Mamie was long and thin. It took quite a few tries, but finally she pushed hard enough that the handcuffs sprang open.

Throwing the handcuffs down, she looked at the clock.

Only twenty minutes remained.

She had to get her legs untied from these tight knots.

Her fingers were stiff and it was too difficult to manage the tight ropes.

Only a tiny light peeked through the tiny window near the ceiling. She watched it for a long while, the darkness hovering, watching.

A different kind of fear than Raz had ever known

grabbed hold: a chilling, tingly, clammy kind of fear. It's cold tendrils wrapped around her ankles and crept up her spine to the back of her neck.

She wanted to run, but the ropes were knotted tight around her ankles. She screamed but to her own ears the sound didn't reach much than her own ears.

How long before someone realized she was missing? Would they be able to find her in time?

Razelle remembered her husband's warm kisses. She realized that she loved him and wanted to stay alive to make their marriage real. She wanted to live a long life together with him.

She came to a new awareness in that moment. Her biggest longing, to guard her heart from pain and hurt, wasn't as important as what she really needed. Which was to be loved by her husband.

She wanted to be loved by Luke.

In this moment, Razelle realized that she would willingly give up her need to have walls around her heart, to live everyday with the man she loved.

Right now, Luke had pulled himself back from getting close to her, but she had confidence he would do everything he could to rescue her once again.

Luke, please come quickly.

It was only a couple minutes later when she heard loud footsteps hurrying down the basement steps.

"Raz, where are you?" Luke turned the corner at the bottom of the stairs, and seeing her ran toward her.

He leaned down to embrace her and his lips landed on hers, like a starving man.

She pushed back trying to talk to him. "I'm so happy to

see you Luke, but we only have three minutes to get out of here. If you help me untie the ropes around my ankles and get us out of here, I promise you can kiss me to your heart's content."

Luke looked at the clock and began hurrying. "Sorry. Yes let's do that. Or better yet, I have a pocket knife with me." With a few quick slashes at the rope, Luke managed to untie her legs.

"Let's go!" Luke grabbed her hand and Raz hurried to keep up with him as they ran up the stairs and out of the house.

They ran until they reached the road, when suddenly a loud explosion pierced their ears.

It shook the earth, and they both fell down.

Razelle sat up, her mouth falling open at the sight of the sight of the house. Dust flew everywhere and the house now lay on the ground in a pile of shattered and broken wood and dirt.

"That could've been me. I could've been part of that shattered pile of debris." Astonishment sucked the air out of her lungs as she stared at the burning house.

Luke's eyes were wide his voice shook as he spoke. "That farm house is gone for good."

The sound of sirens sounded nearby and soon the police arrived. Luke and Razelle both answered a few questions, before they were free to go.

"I've booked us a hotel in town. I need to get you somewhere so you can rest from this terrible day." Luke helped her into the car and drove to town. As if by unspoken agreement, they were silent until they reached their hotel room.

Luke closed the door behind him and looked at her, blinking and motionless for a moment.

Razelle stared at her husband, noticing that the hard line of his jaw didn't conceal the haunted look in his eyes.

Suddenly, he reached for her. "That could've been you, crushed and broken. You could've died. I could've lost you forever."

He kissed her forehead, her eyelids, her cheeks her nose and finally his lips captured hers in hungry need. His lips pulled and devoured hers, like he couldn't get enough.

Luke swallowed back the emotion that threatened to consume him. He sat down, drained.

Razelle let her husband pull her onto his lap, raining kisses on her eyelids and cheeks. "I finally realized today when I nearly lost you, how much you mean to me."

"Oh, Luke." Razelle whispered, her mouth so close to his that their breath mingled. "I'm here now. I'm safe. You saved me."

She reached a hand up and touched his cheek, peering into her husband's haunted eyes.

He nodded, but his eyes still seemed pained, refusing to leave her face.

Then ever so slowly, almost as if he expected her to pull away, Luke moved his lips closer to hers. "I can't stand the thought of losing you. You are my world."

Razelle turned her face to accept his kiss, unable to deny him anything.

LUKE COULD FEEL his chest heaving as he opened his eyes to gaze at Razelle.

Trying to shut out the vivid images of seeing her bound in that chair in the basement, with the count down timer and attached to explosives that would have sent her to an early grave.

He stroked her hair and he released jagged breaths.

"Heaven help me Razelle, but once I realized Maggie Dillan took you to Texas to her Granddad's old farmhouse, I couldn't get to you fast enough."

He stared at her and expelled a breath, shutting his eyes for a brief moment. "At first I thought Maggie would have taken you to Moorea Island, because that's the place you and her lived. But when I asked around, no one had seen you there."

Razelle blinked in confusion.

He'd called around trying to find her. He'd been crazy with worry.

"But then I talked to your Dad. I asked him where he thought Maggie would have taken you. At that moment, he remembered Maggie had inherited her Granddad's old farm and ranch house here in Texas. He was certain Maggie would have taken you there."

Raz sighed in relief. "And you found me. I'm so grateful you came for me, Luke. Thank you." Tears filled her shining green eyes.

He tangled his hands in her thick brown hair, holding her captive, his lips ravaging hers with an intensity that sent her senses reeling. Nothing mattered in this moment, except the warmth of her touch. A fierce tenderness rose up on the inside as Luke fervently fed his need for his wife.

Luke's whispered a heartfelt yearning from deep inside. "My sweet wife. I can't lose you."

"You won't. I'm here. I'm here." His wife's body molded to his and she offered her sweet lips to his once more. Over and over he kissed her, until she was breathless.

Razelle reached up, her arms encircling his neck drawing him closer.

He felt her devotion, and his heart echoed with the same emotion. His heart basked in the realization that she needed him as much as he needed her.

Luke pulled his mouth from hers, with a low moan, as if unwilling to part from her for one moment. His strong arms cradled her close to his chest, and she could hear the rapid beating of his heart. A deep sense of happiness and contentment filled her.

Her husband continued to stroke her hair and Razelle snuggled closer to his heart.

Somewhere in the reality of almost losing his wife, Luke realized that he'd lost his heart to her.

BEING HELD in Luke's arms sent wonderful sensations through her body.

His embrace and his incredible kisses had always sent her reeling, but there was something even more powerful about the tender way her husband held her in his arms at this moment.

Today, she sensed a deeper connection to Luke, almost like they had bonded in a way they hadn't before.

Her husband had told her that he'd become attached to her, but it was only now that she'd finally believed him.

Razelle swallowed back the emotion lodged in her throat.

They sat together in the stillness for a long time, and she cherished this time of closeness with her husband.

"I'm sorry for how I've pushed you away for so long." Luke's gruff whisper broke through the stillness of the moment.

"I told you about losing my ex-fiance, but I've finally realized that all that pain made me too afraid to love someone else. A big part of what has held me back is my own fear of losing another woman I love."

She felt the weight of Luke's sorrow.

"It's okay, Luke." Raz tightened her grip around his waist, aware of how difficult it must be for him to speak of past pain of losing his Dad and later losing his ex-fiance.

Luke's body tensed. "No it's not okay, Razelle. Don't you see? I failed to truly love and protect Audra the way she needed me to. What if I fail you too?"

"You protected me today, Luke. You are the one who saved me from dying in that house explosion." Razelle put her hands on either side of his face trying to convince her husband of the truth of her words.

Luke nodded. "And I'm so thankful I got there in time. But with all my past mistakes and failures, I don't know if the fact that I saved you today, makes up for the many times I've failed."

Razelle could feel the sorrow in her husband's words. Somehow she had to convince him of the truth. "Luke, it wasn't your fault that Audra decided to leave you at the altar.

"And it wasn't your fault your ex-fiance passed away a few weeks later." She moved back a little ways to look into Luke's eyes, her own cloudy with unshed tears.

"But it was my fault. Even though she left me, I should have checked on her. I knew she struggled with depression." Luke pressed his eyes shut, a harsh groan falling from his lips.

"For years, the weight of my dad's death and later Audra's death has all but crushed me. I'm terrified that somehow I'll repeat the same mistakes with you, because I love you so much that it scares me to live day after day without you by my side."

Luke expelled a labored breath. "But I've decided to stop hiding in fear. I want to spend a lifetime learning how to love you better, Razelle."

A single tear slipped down her cheek. He reached over and with gentle fingers wiped them away.

She turned to look into Luke's eyes.

"You love me?"

"I have for weeks. I think I fell in love with you when we went to the camp after the Charity Gala. When the guard grabbed you, I thought I'd lost you and I realized I was deeply, madly in love with you Razelle."

"That also explains why I've been so bad-tempered all these weeks as I've tried my best to push you away and ignore these feelings." Luke ran a shaky hand through his hair, a sheepish expression on his lips. "Sorry about that."

Razelle relished hearing her husband's words of love. "I forgive you. I love you too, with all my heart."

Luke pulled her closer, his lips touching hers briefly. "I've been drawn to you from the first. You're a woman who is kind, gentle and compassionate."

"You are also someone who also happens to be self-less, beautiful and quite captivating." Luke faltered on the last word, as his eyes darkened and moved down to her lips.

She swallowed back emotion at his words, forcing herself to meet his gaze.

His whispered words mingled close to her lips. "I want to kiss you so badly right now, but first I need to know something."

"What do you need to know?"

He paused for a moment. "We agreed that ours would be a fake marriage to benefit us both. But tonight both of us realize we've fallen in love."

Luke leaned his forehead against hers and his eyes squeezed shut, expelling a shuddered breath. He hesitated a moment before he spoke again. "What would you think of being married for real... to a man like me?"

A shaky smile formed on her lips and she released the breath she'd been holding.

Her husband's love for her combined with his need to have her as his forever wife was what she needed to hear to make this marriage real. "Luke you are a wonderful man. You've saved me, you've trusted me with the most vulnerable part of yourself and you've honored me with your love. More than anything, I would be proud to be your wife in every way."

She shivered with anticipation at the tender passion she saw in his eyes.

Softly she whispered. "I love you, Luke."

Her husband's lips touched her own with a sweet reckless abandon. Luke's arms tightened around her and he rolled her so she was lying on her back.

His hands reached up to cradle her face, dark hazel eyes searching hers, a hesitation in his movements.

Razelle leaned over and brushed her lips against his, her kisses saying much more than words ever could.

He groaned, unable to wait a second longer and folded her in his arms, kissing her with the hunger of a starved man. "Razelle my beautiful wife. I can't believe you are mine. Let me show you how much I love you."

Then Luke kissed her again, leaving her with no doubt that their fake marriage had now become very real… and was a forever kind of love.

*ne month later...*

Luke blinked back tears as his beautiful bride came into view at last.

Razelle walked with one hand tucked inside the curve of her Dad's arm and the other on her Mom's arm.

They walked along the grassy knoll toward the beach with a family bond of new beginnings and love radiating between them.

It was quite wonderful to see all of them together.

The setting sun's red-golden hue weaved a shimmering path across the lake, like a mirror reflection of the hair that flowed in loose waves down his bride's back.

When Razelle first came up with the idea that they have another wedding ceremony, this time for real, Luke hadn't been too sure of the idea.

Another ceremony went against his introverted tendency to avoid the spotlight. Yet, when he'd seen how happy Raz was with the idea, he realized he wanted to do whatever he could to please her.

Boone and Millie Donovan were thrilled with the idea of another wedding ceremony. They didn't want to miss any more of their only daughter's important moments.

Razelle longed for her real father and mother to give her away in marriage to the man she loved.

The setting for their vow renewal was perfect.

Boone and Millie Donovan's lakefront property was the same spot Razelle, or Rosalyn as her parents called her, had discovered who she really was. This place gave her a sense of belonging and unwavering love.

This was a perfect beginning for them both.

Razelle had invited some friends she knew from her time at the coffee shop and of course they had asked Addy, Olivia and Cindi to their wedding day.

The girls were all living at the Stevenson Safe House and had round the clock help for anything they needed. One of the workers from the Safe House had driven them here.

A couple of his friends also came to their wedding. Luke was grateful for their support.

Now that Waylon had agreed to be the Director of the Safe House, he was finding new purpose and meaning.

Luke's Mom, Grandmom and brothers all stood near him grinning from ear to ear.

His youngest brother Zach stood by his side as best man. Hudson, Sawyer and Waylon all smiled from their front seats wearing dopey grins, a true testament of their love for their sister who they believed had been lost forever.

He couldn't help but grin at Zach whose eyes were riveted on the maid of honor as she made her way toward them.

Cassie looked beautiful in a pink cocktail length dress. Her raven colored hair was piled high on her head with tiny baby's breath flowers weaved around her hair in a crown.

Luke looked forward to teasing Zach later.

When at last Razelle stepped onto the sandy beach, her green eyes shimmering brightly at him as he stood frozen in place, convinced he was looking at a little bit of heaven on earth.

She wore a long wedding dress that was an A-line gown in ivory colored silk that hugged her slender figure.

It had been Millie Donovan's wedding dress years ago. Razelle had wanted to honor her real Mom by wearing her dress today.

Seeing her now, nobody would be able to tell that only a month ago, his wife had barely escaped an explosion that had been so close to ending her life.

Luke shuddered as he remembered that day in vivid clarity.

Maggie Dillan, the woman who had raised Raz and whom she had believed to be her Mother, had been caught by the Police right after the house explosion.

She was now behind bars.

He sent a prayer of thanks heavenward, grateful his wife was now safe from the lies and deadly plots of that woman.

"Who gives this woman to be married to this man?" The pastor began.

Boone Donovan's voice was tender as he looked at his daughter. "Her mother and I." Millie leaned over placing a gentle kiss on Razelle's cheek. Boone followed suit, placing Razelle's hand in Luke's.

He swallowed back emotion at the tender moment between them.

His bride quickly wiped away tears before tucking her hand inside his.

The pastor spoke and this time when they repeated their marriage vows, they were given with depth and meaning.

They were committing to love each other for life.

His bride's green eyes filled with tears and seemed to stare deep into his soul.

In the beginning he hadn't wanted a real marriage, but since he fell in love with Razelle it seemed he couldn't wait for this moment.

No longer would their marriage be one of convenience. After today, they would have a real marriage based on love and commitment.

Gently, he reached for her. With his arms around her waist, he lowered his head and gently placed his lips on hers.

The sweetness of her kiss intoxicated him. He breathed her in deeply, loving the way her arms held tightly to him.

Having his bride in his arms, felt like coming home.

RAZELLE'S KNEES weakened and her pulse quickened as Luke's warm lips pressed against her own.

Her arms slipped further around his waist holding tightly to her husband. Love had melted her heart and turned her emotions into a gooey, messy puddle.

She loved every second.

It had been so incredible to find a husband who would love her like this. This kind of love had been on her list from the beginning, but she never really thought it would happen for her.

Believing that she wasn't worthy to be loved and that she, a person others needed to pity, had all been lies. Those lies had created wounds in her heart where she had put up walls.

She saw that clearly now.

Maggie, the woman who raised her, had tried to convince her that Luke or any man wouldn't accept her as she was.

Her husband's acceptance and love had proven that to be a lie.

Luke really did love her. He didn't pity her or feel sorry for her.

He had wanted her to embrace who she was meant to be and to live everyday in a new freedom.

And now Razelle truly belonged to a family again. For so long she had felt lost and displaced, unsure why she felt that way.

Discovering her real family had meant she was confident in who she really was.

Now, she not only had a real family of her own, but she was also part of the Stevenson family.

Marrying Luke had shifted everything. Now they were part of a bigger family that they belonged to. It was the most wonderful feeling in the world.

Her heart overflowed with contentment.

Luke ended the kiss, his eyes flickering with tenderness.

When he pulled his arms away, Razelle sighed missing her husband's warmth.

They were announced as husband and wife amid much clapping and cheers.

"We've decided to change the rules for gifts for our wedding. We thought instead of giving gifts to us, you could give a small donation to the new center for teenagers that we're building." Luke smiled over at her.

"My wife has a passion to help teenagers who come from a life on the streets, to find healing and help so they can get back to a normal healthy life as productive members of society." Luke's unexpected announcement was greeted with cheers from family and friends alike.

Raz had been surprised and excited when Luke had originally mentioned that he wanted to build the center for struggling teenagers.

It was something she had longed to do ever since she had first visited the camp and experienced the struggles there.

She whispered softly. "Thank you for doing that. I'm excited for when it opens. It's going to be an incredible help up for those who need it."

"I'm just happy it's something we can do together."

"I love that." She slipped her hand in his. While their

guests were busy talking with one another, Luke and Razelle walked to where the sand touched the water.

"I was going to surprise you, but I can't wait."

"What is it?"

"I thought we would fly back to Moorea Island to visit your Grandmere, sort of as a second honeymoon."

"Oh Luke, that would be amazing."

"Good. I need you rested up for when the work begins on our new ranch house." He chuckled, his eyes crinkling with playfulness.

"I'll be plenty ready to get the designs figured out for the ranch house as well as the center for teenagers, don't you worry." Razelle was excited that so many of her dreams were coming true.

He laughed out loud at her eagerness.

"Oh Luke. Thank you for remembering Mamie. I can't wait to see her." Her eyes glistened with tears and she reached up to kiss him on the cheek.

"Thank you for being so thoughtful. Even before we were husband and wife for real, you always thought of me first. I appreciate that."

"Well I've learned how important it is to have the love of family. You taught me that." He pulled her close, slipping both arms around her.

They stood there for a long time, looking at the sunset on the lake.

"This is the same spot you discovered who you are and learned about your real family." Luke's warm breath whispered on top of her head.

"Yes." The corners of her mouth turned up as happy memories of that day came back. "Most of all I remember how you stuck by me, accepting me as I was, even through my confusion and fear. Thank you."

Luke pulled her close. "We've both had fears and misconceptions. I'm grateful we've chosen to accept and love each other instead."

Her husband moved and placed both hands on her cheeks, looking deeply into her eyes.

"Making that marriage barter was the best thing I ever did, because it brought me you. I… I love you."

A single tear rolled down her cheek at his words. Her husband still stuttered when he felt deep emotions.

She would never get tired of that — or of hearing his words of love.

"And I love you."

EPILOGUE

ach

BILLIONAIRE ZACH STEVENSON, is handsome and in great demand for his skills as a well known yacht designer and builder of boats all along the west coast.

He's got almost everything he's dreamed of, except the one thing he wants most: *Walker's Cove Marina.*

There's only one obstacle standing in his way: Great Grandfather's will stipulates he must marry by his 27th birthday to receive his inheritance.

He only has 3 weeks until the deadline.

Cassie White escaped life with her self-absorbed step-mother in Seattle, Washington to live with her dad's brother, Doc White.

It doesn't take long for her to settle in, living and

working with her uncle and his six friends at the edge of the small town of Paradise Lake.

Cassie feels safe in the large old Victorian cottage until suddenly one day, someone goes to great lengths to try to hurt her.

Now, she is afraid and desperate for help.

Will being forced together tear Zach and Cassie apart, or throw them towards true love?

❧

Ready To Read the Next Story in This Series? Start Reading Zach's Story Today!

Billionaire Zach Stevenson, is handsome and in demand for his skills as a well known yacht designer and builder of boats all along the west coast. He's got almost everything he's dreamed of, except the one thing he wants most: *Walker's Cove Marina.*

Only one obstacle stands in his way: *Great Grandfather's will stipulates he must marry by his 27th birthday to receive his inheritance. He only has 3 weeks until the deadline.*

Cassie White escaped life with her self-absorbed stepmother in Seattle, Washington to live with her dad's brother, Doc White. It doesn't take long for her to settle in, living and working with her uncle and his six friends at the edge of the small town of Paradise Lake.

Cassie feels safe in the large old Victorian cottage until suddenly one day, someone goes to great lengths to try to hurt her. Now, she is afraid and desperate for help. *Will being forced together tear Zach and Cassie apart, or throw them towards true love?*

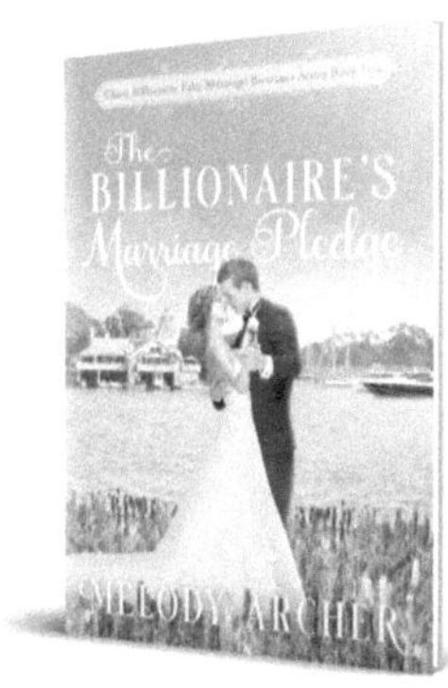

Clean Billionaire Fake Marriage Romance Series

Book 1: The Billionaire's Marriage Bargain

Book 2: The Billionaire's Marriage Contract

Book 3: The Billionaire's Marriage Promise

Book 4: The Billionaire's Marriage Barter

Book 5: The Billionaire's Marriage Pledge

7 Brides for 7 Cowboys, Small Town Sweet Western Romance Series

Book 1: The Forgiven Cowboy's Best Friend

Book 2: The Redeemed Cowboy's Secret Baby

Book 3: The Honorable Cowboy's Convenient Marriage

Book 4: Pre-Order The Wounded Cowboy's Beauty Bride

Books 5, 6 & 7 *Still to Come...*

Find your favorite Sweet Romance series on my New Author Website. *Grab your book at a discount when you buy direct(use code: MFB10).*

www.MemorableFictionBooks.com

ABOUT THE AUTHOR

Melody Archer lives in Alberta with her husband and their four young adults.

Recently, her oldest son married his wife from Brazil. Their family has really enjoyed getting to know their new daughter-in-law.

She loves new and classic romantic movies, green smoothies and going on adventures with her family.

Melody would love to connect with you :)

facebook.com/melodyarcherauthor

instagram.com/melodyarcherauthor

bookbub.com/profile/melody-archer